INJECTING
FAITH

A Dr. Beckett Campbell Medical Examiner
Thriller

Book 2

Patrick Logan

Books by Patrick Logan

Detective Damien Drake

Book 1: Butterfly Kisses (feat. Chase Adams, Dr. Campbell)
Book 2: Cause of Death (feat. Chase Adams, Dr. Campbell)
Book 3: Download Murder (feat. Chase Adams, Dr. Campbell)
Book 4: Skeleton King (feat. Dr. Campbell)
Book 5: Human Traffic (feat. Dr. Campbell)
Book 6: Drug Lord: Part I
Book 7: Drug Lord: Part II

Chase Adams FBI Thrillers

Book 1: Frozen Stiff
Book 2: Shadow Suspect
Book 3: Drawing Dead
Book 4: Amber Alert
Book 4.5: Georgina's Story
Book 5: Dirty Money
Book 6: Devil's Den

Dr. Beckett Campbell Medical Thrillers

Book 0: Bitter End
Book 1: Organ Donor
Book 2: Injecting Faith
Book 3: Surgical Precision

INJECTING FAITH

Prologue

"COME ON IN AND TAKE a seat, please," the woman said, as she herself took up residence in a comfortable oversized chair. The boy followed suit but kept his head low the entire time, refusing to meet her eyes. He slumped down and crossed his arms over his chest defiantly. "Well, are you going to tell me what happened?"

The boy shook his head.

"Okay, okay, you don't have to talk about it now, but eventually, you're going to have to take responsibility for your actions. This is the third time you've acted up this week. And this time, you gave Charlie a black eye. This type of behavior is not acceptable here; you can't attack people unprovoked. You *know* this."

The boy huffed, his tiny chest rising and falling dramatically beneath his thin arms.

The woman sighed, took her glasses off, and laid them on her lap. She couldn't believe that a boy this young, only five years of age, could have so much pent-up anger inside him. So much hostility. So much unrequited hatred.

"I know it's tough, I know this isn't the life that you're used to, and it's going to take some adjustment. But you can't hit the other kids… and if you don't tell me why you're so upset all the time, I can't help you. And that's what I want to do; I want to help you."

The boy took another deep breath and then opened his mouth to speak. She thought she might finally be getting to him, but his jaw snapped shut and he just shook his head.

"You have to speak, to use your words. Violence won't—"

The boy suddenly lifted his eyes and glared at her.

"I want to kill him," he whispered.

The words were said with such fury, that the woman had to clear her throat before speaking.

"Ex-excuse me?"

"I want to kill him," the boy repeated. "I *need* to kill him.

The next question should have been 'why'—all of the woman's training told her so—but she couldn't resist asking something else.

"*Who*? Kill who? Charlie? Do you want to kill Charlie?"

Another violent headshake.

"Then who are you talking about? This behavior—"

"Not Charlie—I want to kill the man who murdered my dad. I want to kill the man with the blond hair and tattoos."

PART I

Death is a Disease

Chapter 1

"HAVE YOU SEEN *A CLOCKWORK* Orange, Wayne?" Dr. Beckett Campbell asked as he walked around the chair and turned on the projector. It was only about the size of an external hard drive, and when it flickered to life, it put out just enough light to illuminate the concrete wall.

The muffled reply that followed was completely unintelligible.

Beckett went to his computer next and plugged it into the side of the projector. Then he loaded up a video file and pressed play.

"Well, this is kinda like that." He rocked his head from side to side. "Okay, you got me; it's not *really* like *A Clockwork Orange*. I mean, you only have a few things in common with that movie. Like those things spreading your eyelids apart… they're called speculums. They had *those* in the movie—*psst*, it's so you can't blink. Only, in the movie, they used what's called a *Barraquer* speculum. You're right, you're right… it doesn't really matter what it's called, suffice it to say that they're actually quite comfortable. Ah, but I'm afraid you weren't so lucky—I didn't have any of those fancy doodads handy. So, I fashioned your speculums out of a couple of coat hangers I had lying around."

Again, more protests from behind the strip of tape covering the man's mouth. Beckett paused as the video booted up and the opening scene played out. It was a beach setting, at first only showing rolling waves and soft sand that looked incredibly warm and inviting, given the cool New York City fall outside. But then a child came into view, a young boy sporting only blue swim trunks and running away from the camera. He was laughing, showing off new front teeth that had barely started to grow in.

"Soon, your eyes are going to get incredibly dry. Trust me, you're going to hate it. You are going to beg for eyedrops, you would do anything for a splash of water on them. I'm not going to give anything to you, of course, but trust me, it's going to feel like your eyes were once plump, juicy grapes and now they're desiccated prunes. It has to be one of the most uncomfortable sensations imaginable… but I digress. Oh, this is another thing you have in common with *A Clockwork Orange;* you're gonna watch a film. Meta, isn't it?"

The man hissed into his tape, but Beckett paid him no heed. On screen, the camera nestled into the sand and a man came into view, chasing his son.

"But the main difference?" Beckett continued. "In that movie, in the book as well, but most people don't read the books anymore—let's be honest, who has time to read books when you've got podcasts, Amazon Prime, and Netflix? *Nobody,* that's who. Anyways, in *A Clockwork Orange*, the main character—his name is Alex, FYI—is healed in the end."

Beckett paused for effect and the scene on the projector changed. They were transported to a snowy setting. The little boy was skating, and he was actually pretty good for an eight-year-old. It was apparent, though, when he crashed into a snow bank, that he was still working on his stopping.

"At the end of this movie, however, you won't be healed, Wayne. You'll be dead."

The man's muffled cries intensified, and he tried to shift his head from side to side. He actually managed to move a little, despite the strap that was laced across his forehead and tied to the back of the chair. Taking no chances, Beckett quickly moved behind the man's head and tightened it. Then he picked up a scalpel and walked in front of the man. Wayne's eyes were already on the verge of bulging from his head, but when he saw the shiny blade that Beckett conveniently held in the path of the projector light, they seemed to widen even further. This caused the jagged edges of the makeshift speculums to slice into his bottom eyelids. Bloody tears spilled down the man's pasty cheeks.

"Ah, isn't that cute; but don't cry for me, Argentina. Spoiler Alert: you want to know how I know you'll be dead by the end of the movie?"

Wayne huffed against the tape, his cheeks puffing with every breath.

"Yeah, you guessed it; it's because I'm going to kill you."

Wayne's breathing became so rapid and his chest heaved so dramatically from beneath his soiled white T-shirt, that Beckett thought he might hyperventilate and go into cardiac arrest.

He better not. He better not fucking die on me.

"What happened to you, Wayne? You were—"

The sound of something dripping surprised Beckett and he immediately looked over at Wayne. Then he started to grin.

A puddle had formed beneath the man's chair.

"Oh, come on. You pissed yourself? Give me a fucking break, Wayne. Ah, never mind—that's okay. It's okay because I put a plastic sheet beneath your chair. I mean, its main purpose is to collect blood, but piss will do, too. Anyways, as I was saying," Beckett pointed at the wall with the scalpel before tapping the dull side against his palm. His fingers were tingling so much now that he could barely feel them. "You were such a cute kid, and yet you turned into such a fucking animal. A *savage*. What happened to you?"

The boy in the video was on a slide, clearly intending on landing on an inflatable swan in the pool below. He overshot his mark and landed in the water instead.

"Such a cute kid... what the fuck happened to you?"

Wayne was trying to speak again, more intent on getting the words out than ever.

Beckett rolled his eyes and grabbed the corner of the tape. He pulled it off with one yank.

"That's—that's—that's n-n-n-not—"

Wayne cried out, but Beckett hushed him.

"To-to-to-day, Junior."

"That's not me, that's not me." Wayne's words came out in a rush. His voice was high-pitched, and slobber dripped onto his chin.

Beckett made a face.

"Keep watching," he instructed.

All of a sudden, the grainy footage became clearer as it transitioned from standard definition to high definition.

But Beckett wasn't interested in the quality of the film.

The video showed a first-person view of a forest now. There were dull gray and brown leaves scattered everywhere, and the sound of footsteps could be heard from Beckett's computer.

"I don't know what—"

"Shh, this is the good part. Or the bad part, depending on how you look at it."

Wayne fell silent.

In addition to the footsteps, there was also heavy breathing, and the camera bounced up and down with every step. Slowly, an item that was partially buried in the leaves came into focus. It was a maroon backpack with the name *Will* stitched on it.

"I can explain—"

Beckett held the scalpel out.

"Not another word, Wayne," he said in a flat tone.

They watched the rest of the video in silence. After the backpack, the video camera zoomed in on a pair of white underwear.

A couple more steps and the naked body of Will Kingston came into the shot. His pale, almost white, buttocks, were sticking out of the leaves, but the top half of his body was buried beneath them. Strands of dirty blond hair were tangled in the dried vegetation, but not much else was visible. The camera operator suddenly dropped to a knee. A hand brushed leaves away from the boy's face, revealing a frozen expression of terror. For a moment, Will's milky eyes seemed to bore into the camera, and with every second this image remained on screen, the tingling in Beckett's fingertips increased.

Slowly, the camera started to turn, stopping only when Wayne Cravat's face filled the frame.

He was grinning, revealing a mouth full of crowded teeth.

"No," Beckett said as he moved in front of Wayne again. "that little boy *wasn't* you; that was one of your victims. Let's be honest, there's no way that something as disgusting as yourself would have been that cute as a child."

Beckett squatted in front of the chair now.

"It's not what it looks like... I didn't—I didn't—"

Beckett reached out and pressed a finger to the man's lips.

"*Yech.*" Beckett pulled his now slobber-covered finger back and wiped it on Wayne's jeans. Then he leaned forward and drove the scalpel directly into the man's fat neck, just below where his jaw made a forty-five-degree turn and headed north.

Chapter 2

"SHIT," BECKETT GRUMBLED AS HE reached for his phone. His hand was covered in blood, and he did his best to wipe most of it off on Wayne's already soiled T-shirt. It had been ringing off the hook for the past ten minutes, which meant that it could only be one person.

"Hi there," he said.

"What are you up to tonight?" a female voice asked.

Beckett looked down at Wayne's corpse and the blood that continued to leak out of him. His heart had stopped more than five minutes ago, but the man was so fat that his blood just kept oozing out of the wound on his neck. There was so much blood, in fact, that Beckett was starting to become concerned that the plastic cloth he'd put down wouldn't contain it all, especially considering it was half full of piss.

"Oh, you know, reading textbooks and speaking to colleagues on *Reddit* about the newest scientific advancements," he said with a nerdy accent.

"Yeah, right. Seriously, what are you up to tonight?"

Beckett stared at Wayne's eyes that were still pried open by the pieces of coat hanger.

"I'll probably just listen to an episode of *Casefile* and have a scotch. Nothing special. You?"

"You're turning into an old man, you know that?"

Beckett placed the scalpel that he was still holding in the dish with the other tools and let it soak in the alcohol.

"Guilty as charged. I'm thirty-five years old, but I've got the body of an octogenarian. A ripped, 'roided to the gills, eighty-year-old. What's up, Suzan? You don't call me for small talk. Is this a booty call? Because I feel used. I'm not just a piece of meat, you know."

"Speaking of meat, I'm tired and hungry from studying. We could do dinner. You know, like normal people."

Beckett raised an eyebrow.

Normal… I was normal once, wasn't I?

"Yeah, I don't—"

Beckett heard a chime from high above him.

That's weird, I could've sworn I turned off the TV.

"Too late. I'm bringing over Chinese."

Now it was Beckett's eyes that went wide.

"Suzan, I'm—"

Another chime.

"Where the fuck are you, anyway? The food's getting cold."

Beckett swallowed hard.

"I'm at the—" *office*, he meant to say, but Suzan cut him off.

"Your lights are on and I know you're home. Just come to the damn door. Don't make me put the food down and get my keys out of my pocket."

"You're… you're *here*? At my house?"

"What's wrong with you? Why do you sound so surprised? You have another woman in there or something?"

No, Beckett thought with a frown. *Not a woman, but a corpse… the corpse of a man I just killed.*

Chapter 3

SGT. HENRY YASIV PULLED A cigarette out of the pack and brought it to his lips. When he'd picked up smoking again about a year ago, after a five-year layoff, he'd promised himself that when all the problems with the mayor of New York and the whole heroin drug ring mess were resolved, he'd quit.

Of course, even after everyone involved in the ANGUIS Holdings Corporation was either in prison or dead or had fled the country, Yasiv had told himself that he'd quit after his next case.

His next case just happened to be an Army Captain who had been shot dead at his own charity auction moments before the NYPD, including himself, were to issue a warrant for his arrest.

The man had been shot by an unknown assailant on his daughter's back lawn. They had no leads, despite the fact that there were over fifty guests at the auction. But, what with the chaos that ensued with the NYPD's arrival, no one saw anything.

It was a cold case now and was destined to become frozen. Not that he cared. Captain Loomis was involved in distributing carfentanyl-laced heroin throughout the city. It was Yasiv's opinion that the man got what he'd deserved.

So, he'd promised himself that he would quit smoking when he resolved his *next* case.

Yasiv inhaled deeply, relishing the sensation of warm smoke as it entered his lungs. Then he tucked his hands deep into his pockets and buried his neck into the collar of his peacoat.

Global warming might be in full effect, but it appeared to have skipped New York City this year. Only fall, it already felt like February.

It didn't help that he was getting older; that he *felt* older. Sgt. Henry Yasiv was a week from his thirtieth birthday, but he felt twice that number. It showed, too. There were new lines framing his eyes and deep grooves around his nose. He'd even become accustomed to finding a gray hair or two, whenever he got around to brushing it.

But this didn't bother him.

There was a time when Yasiv cared what he looked like, but that was *before;* before Craig Sloan started staging his murders to look like a suicide. There'd been a time when he'd had a keen interest in insects, but that was before Marcus Slasinsky had put caterpillars in the mouths of his victims. Reading had once been a hobby of his, but that was before Ryanne Elliot had written about her murder victims and published the stories online.

Yeah, he was a different man, now. Once, his colleagues, like Chase Adams, now with the FBI, and Damien Drake, now a fugitive and most likely dead, had thought him too green to go anywhere in the department.

It was a crying shame that he'd proven them wrong.

After Chase Adams had vacated the Sergeant post, he'd been appointed in a matter of days. His rise up the ranks of NYPD 62nd division was nothing short of meteoric, but Yasiv wasn't naive; his promotion wasn't based solely on merit.

After the indictments had been handed down, he was one of only a handful of cops left who wasn't dirty.

Yasiv took another heavy drag, enjoying the sound of the cigarette wrapper burning.

He was also young-*ish* and a fresh face. A signal to the people of New York that the corruption that festered within the NYPD for so many years was now gone.

But what they hadn't told him, was that the body count rose the higher up the ranks you went. And yet, with the increase in pressure and responsibility, the more impersonal everything become along the way.

The more *numb*.

The door opened behind him, and Yasiv turned to see Detective Dunbar peering out. Another young, green face.

"Hank? I've got PO Salzman waiting for you."

Yasiv nodded and thanked Dunbar.

"I'll be in in a minute, as soon as I finish my smoke."

Normally, a sergeant wouldn't get involved with a PO violation. Normally, Yasiv would stay as far away from such a minor infraction as possible.

He took a final drag of his cigarette, exhaled a thick cloud of smoke, and then flicked the butt to the curb.

But Wayne Cravat was no normal parolee.

Chapter 4

"OH SHIT, OH SHIT, *OH shit!*" Beckett shouted as he sprinted up the stairs and burst through the basement door. He tried to slam it closed but then had to run back when he realized that it was still ajar. Then he glanced down at himself. He was wearing an apron that was literally covered in blood. He quickly tore it off, then jammed it beneath the sink.

"Beckett?" he heard Suzan say.

Fuck!

His first thought was that he hadn't hung up his phone yet, and he looked at it. The screen was dark, which meant that—

"Beckett?"

—Suzan had used her keys to open the door and was just now stepping inside.

He frantically searched his dark shirt and jeans for any sign of Wayne's blood. Not immediately finding any, he turned to the fridge, knowing that he only had a few seconds before Suzan made her way to the kitchen.

How the hell did this happen?

Beckett could see the headlines now: *Serial Killer Captured because the Moron Gave a Set of Keys to Girlfriend.*

You idiot!

"I'm in here, Shnookums," he hollered.

There wasn't much in the fridge: a handful of beers, some ketchup, mayo, and a block of cheese. With the headaches he'd been experiencing lately, Beckett had lost most of his appetite.

He found two thick-cut sirloin steaks on the bottom shelf and quickly pulled them out. Then he spun around, tossed them on the cutting board on the center island, and tore the plastic off.

"What the heck are you doing?" Suzan asked as she stepped into the kitchen.

Beckett tried his best to offer his girlfriend a natural-looking smile.

He failed miserably; the expression on his face was the one of a man who just sharted and realized he was wearing white cotton pants.

"I was just about to cook some steaks," he said, nodding towards the hunks of meat on the cutting board.

Suzan raised an eyebrow and stared at him. She had this way of seeing through him, a way of penetrating his soul.

The outer layer, at least.

More than ten years his younger, she offered him something that other women he'd dated or slept with over the years couldn't. Mainly, she kept up with him, in more ways than one.

And she kept him in line, too; she didn't put up with his shit as others in the past had.

Some people might frown at their age difference or the fact that she was a TA for one of his residency classes, but Beckett made a habit of not caring what other people thought. Suzan Cuthbert was an adult who could make her own decisions.

Suggesting otherwise was just plain ignorant.

"And did you slaughter the cow yourself?" she asked as she set the two bags of takeout down on the table.

He shook his head.

Not a cow, exactly.

"Then why are you sweating?"

"IBS," he replied quickly.

Suzan looked at him and crinkled her nose.

"I told you that I got takeout."

She was a good five inches shorter than Beckett, so when she leaned up to kiss him, it was on him to do most of the heavy lifting. Their lips met, but only for a second; Beckett was worried she'd be able to smell the death on him.

When Suzan pulled away and looked up at him with her green eyes, Beckett held her stare. She was an extrovert who liked to be in the presence of others, but she was also introspective, smart, intellectually curious, sexy as hell, fit, funny, crude, sarcastic, had an ass like the North Star, tits like—

He blinked and averted his eyes.

Jesus, you'd think you were in love, Beckett.

"Yeah, but I was already getting things ready when you called," he lied. "I was going to vacuum seal the steaks, sous vide them for about an hour and then sear at ultra-high heat on the cast-iron."

Suzan made a face.

"Who are you and what have you done with Beckett?"

"It's a new era, Suzan," Beckett said agonizingly slowly. "Women can vote and men can cook. Didn't you hear?"

Suzan rolled her eyes.

"Yeah, but men still can't seem to be able to pee in the toilet."

The comment took Beckett by surprise and he needed a moment to process it.

"You smell like piss, like a homeless man."

Fucking Wayne.

Beckett took a deep breath and tried to play it cool.

"Well, you know what they say… sprinkles are for cupcakes and toilet seats… and underwear. Something like that, anyway."

Suzan went back to the table and started taking the food out of the bags.

"No one says that."

"Sure, they do."

"No, they don't. Put the steaks away, we'll cook them tomorrow, Gordon Ramsay."

"Yes, ma'am."

Beckett re-wrapped the meat and put it back in the fridge. When he turned back, he was surprised to see that Suzan was staring at him again.

"The modern man... can't pee in the toilet and can't do his own laundry, either."

"What?"

Suzan pointed to the back of his shirt and Beckett craned his neck.

"You got blood on your shirt," she informed him.

Beckett's heart did a triple axel in his chest.

"I can see that," he somehow managed. There was a quarter-sized drop of Wayne's blood on the hem of his shirt, and more on his jeans beneath.

"Must've been from the steaks," he offered.

"Oh, really, Mr. Sous vide? For someone so experienced in the kitchen, I'm surprised that you're unaware of the fact that there is no blood in meat from a properly butchered animal."

"Maybe the butcher was drunk then, or perhaps I just cut myself shaving," Beckett shot back as he grabbed a couple of plates from the shelf and brought them over. He just started to open a metal takeout container when Suzan knocked his hand away.

Beckett's eyes narrowed.

"What? What is it now?"

"Go wash your hands, Mr. IBS. *Gross.*"

Chapter 5

"So, PO Salzman, I've just got a couple questions for you," Yasiv said as he slid into the seat across from the man. He opened the folder that Dunbar had prepared for him and turned his attention to the pages within.

"Am I in some sort of trouble?"

Yasiv lifted his eyes to look at the man. He had shaggy dark hair, a beard that extended a little too far down his neck, and had red-rimmed eyes, either from too much alcohol or not enough sleep.

Maybe both.

"No," Yasiv said, shaking his head. "Why would you think that?"

Salzman shrugged and glanced around.

"Normally, when a police sergeant invites you for an interview, sits you down in one of the chairs usually reserved for suspects or prisoners, and has a folder in front of him, you're in trouble."

"Normally? Do you mean that this has happened to you before?"

Salzman looked at Dunbar who was standing behind him, arms crossed over his chest, then turned back to Yasiv.

"No, not to me... but it happens in just about every cop movie I've ever seen. Oh, and please call me Tully—my dad went by Salzman."

Yasiv nodded.

"All right, Tully. No, you're not in trouble. I just have a couple questions for you about one of your charges."

Tully sighed.

"When you called me in I thought either I was in trouble or it was about Wayne. Fifty-fifty, I figured."

Yasiv stared at Tully, trying to get a read of what he was all about. In his limited experience, PO officers were usually as bad as the cons they were in charge of. Parole Officers held an incredible amount of power over their charges and, well, everyone knows the Spiderman dogma. Too bad being responsible wasn't a prerequisite for the job.

But Tully Salzman seemed different; he just seemed like a regular guy.

"Well, I've documented everything," Salzman informed him. "I put it all right there in the report." He raised his eyes and peered across the table at the folder in front of Yasiv. "Yeah, it's there. Wayne was supposed to check in last week, but he missed it. I didn't report it—it's only his first infraction and I believe in second chances—but after he missed yesterday, I flagged him. Other than that, he's been a model parolee."

"Second chances?" Dunbar asked incredulously from the back of the room. Salzman turned to look at him, his eyes narrowing.

"Yeah, second chances. Look, I'm not condoning anything that asshole has done, but if we are gonna let him out on parole, second chances are—"

"More like fifth or sixth chances," Dunbar interrupted. This was a new side of Dunbar. If anything, he could count on Dunbar for being jovial, not ornery. But this was different. For some reason, this case struck a nerve with the man.

Yasiv made a mental note to keep an eye on him.

He cleared his throat.

"This isn't a witch hunt. We're not blaming you for anything, but I'll be the first to admit that I'm getting some kinda pressure from up high. After the fallout from the whole Ken Smith mayor debacle, the DA doesn't want any press at the moment. And Wayne Cravat not showing up for his scheduled meeting with his PO, especially given the brutal nature of the crimes that he was accused of? *Definitely* press worthy. The DA wants him back in custody before the man's face is plastered all over the news… *again.*"

"I don't know where he is."

"You don't know? How could you—"

"Dunbar, take a walk," Yasiv said, trying to bury his frustration. Dunbar's attitude wasn't helping any.

The man glared at him, and for a moment, Yasiv thought that he was going to disobey a direct order. But then he unlaced his arms and left the interview room in a huff.

Yasiv waited for the door to close behind him before continuing.

"As you can see, everyone's got their back up about this. Most people think that he's guilty of killing little Will Kingston, irrespective of the jury's decision."

Tully nodded.

"Yeah, I get it. But here's the thing, you think I choose my parolees? You think I wanted to oversee Wayne Cravat? Given the horrible things he was accused of? Hell no."

Yasiv bit his lower lip.

"Yeah, I know. And you obviously had nothing to do with his acquittal or the fact that he's now missing, but the sad reality is, people are going to hold you responsible in one way or another. Fair, unfair, whatever, it is what it is."

Tully scratched his neck beard.

"Who knows? Maybe he offed himself like Trent did. Would save me a lot of paperwork."

Yasiv's brow furrowed and Tully pressed on.

"Winston Trent? Two hung juries for the murder of Bentley Thomas? Anyway, the best they could do was get him on showing lewd material to a minor or some shit. I was his PO too before he went and offed himself. Like I said before, I'm all for second chances, but if your second chance means that you want to off yourself?" he shrugged. "I'm okay with that, too."

Yasiv looked down at the papers that Dunbar had compiled for him. Sure enough, the second page was for Winston Trent.

"So, is this selection process random, then? I mean, who gets assigned to you? If so, you got a stroke of bad luck these past few months."

"Is it random? It's supposed to be," Tully began, "but it's not, not really. The thing is, some of the other POs..."

He let his sentence trail off, but it wasn't good enough for Yasiv.

"These POs what?"

"I don't want to be that guy," Tully said suddenly, obviously conflicted.

Yasiv understood.

"Hey, we're looking for Wayne Cravat, that's it. If there's anything you might be able to help us with..."

"Whatever. Look, they say it's random, but the truth is, some of the other POs? They're one step up from a DMV clerk. They wouldn't know how to deal with a guy like Wayne or Winston. Winston in particular. He's a master manipulator. If he was assigned to one of the douchebag POs who is either high or drunk all the time? He'd be able to get away with anything. I guess my boss just knows I won't put up with that shit."

"And yet you gave Wayne a pass when he missed his last appointment."

"Yeah, I did, I'll admit it, but I didn't break any rules. If it were Winston? I would report his ass immediately; that guy was a piece of work. Wayne is different; I mean, I know there's a lot of hostility toward the man, but he was acquitted of murdering the Kingston boy, and not in the way that Winston got off. You should read Wayne's file—he's not like the others. I'm not saying he's Mother Teresa or Gandhi, but still. Never caught a break, that guy. Not ever. Anyways, the thing is, I knew where he was the whole time: he was at home."

"And how did you know that?" Yasiv asked. The truth was that he knew little about Wayne Cravat. If it weren't for the DA shoving this case in his face, he would have liked to keep it that way, too.

"Because regardless of how I feel about him, the last thing I wanted was for a man with his history to be on the loose. So, I swung by his place and did a little knocking. I didn't see him, but there was something on the stove. Figured he was taking a shit or something. I gave him until the next PO visit, which was only two days after his missed appointment before I flagged him. Which is what I did. I mean, I'd appreciate if you didn't go over my head on this, but I'll stand by what I did. Obviously, I regret it now, but I'll stand by my decision."

Yasiv nodded and rose to his feet. On the face of it, Wayne Cravat going missing looked bad. But so far as he could tell, Tully was a good man.

He held out his hand, and the PO shook it.

"Thanks for coming in, Tully. Like I said, I'm getting pressure from above, I don't want to make it seem like I'm just coming down on you."

"Yeah, I get it, everything has gone to shit since that whole Ken Smith thing went down. Anyways, if you have any other questions, I'd prefer that you come to me first, and not my boss, if you know what I mean." Tully started toward the door. "You know, professional courtesy and all that."

"Sure thing." Yasiv opened the door. "You know your way out?"

Tully nodded.

"Yeah, see you around, Sgt. Yasiv."

Yasiv nodded and watched the man leave. No sooner had Tully Salzman disappeared down the hallway, did Detective Dunbar appear by Yasiv's side.

"You believe that fucking guy? He lets someone like Wayne Cravat run rampant in *our* city? If that pervert so much as jaywalks, it's on him."

Yasiv turned to Detective Dunbar and inspected him closely.

"Let it go, Dunbar. He's just trying to do his job."

"Yeah, well, he should do his job better. He should do his job a *lot* better."

Chapter 6

THE CHINESE WASN'T HALF BAD. Personally, Beckett would've preferred the steaks, but all in all, the food was serviceable.

"Thanks for picking up dinner," he said as he dabbed his mouth and took their plates to the sink. He dropped them in and then turned back to face Suzan. She was eyeballing him again. "What? What is it this time?"

"I made dinner, so you have to do the dishes. And no, just putting them in the sink doesn't count, Beckett."

He grinned.

"Oh, aren't you a progressive woman. I'll do them later; there's something I want to talk to you about first."

Normally, Suzan wouldn't let this slide. The irony of their relationship was that while Beckett was older, she was the mature one. But he'd caught her attention, mature or not, she was a woman and therefore could not resist a *talk*.

Only, Beckett doubted that she was going to enjoy this one very much.

"Yeah? What is it?"

Beckett glanced around the room.

"Hey? Where'd it go?"

"Where did what go?"

Beckett didn't answer; he was too busy racking his brain for where he might've left it.

In the basement? Tell me I didn't leave it in the fucking basement.

"Wait, before you get it, whatever *it* is, I just want to make sure that you know I prefer BMWs to Mercedes, okay?" Suzan joked with a grin.

Beckett was so lost in thought that he barely heard her. He kept thinking about the basement, the projector, Wayne Cravat, and whether or not he'd taken the damn newspaper down there.

"Beckett? You getting one of your headaches again?"

He snapped his fingers and turned toward the drawer to the left of the stove. He yanked it open and pulled out the newspaper.

"Here it is," Beckett exclaimed. He tossed it to Suzan who somehow managed to catch it against her chest.

"Gee, thanks. You make a girl feel so special," she remarked as she looked at the front page.

"I was thinking about that vacation I owe you," Beckett began. "Seeing what we both went through with the organs and the McEwing disaster and all that jazz."

Suzan's face lifted but then sank again as she read the headline article. She turned the paper around, showing Beckett the photo of the pastor with his arms out to the sides. The one whose head was circled in red had Xs over his eyes, and a comic tongue lolling out, all courtesy of Beckett's Sharpie.

"Montréal," she said simply. "You promised me Montréal."

"I know, I know," Beckett said as he turned his back to her and started to wash the dishes. "It's just that it's cold as balls there, now. I mean, it's probably like minus a hundred Celsius, and nobody knows how cold that is in Fahrenheit. And the *French*… don't get me started on the French. I say we go somewhere warm, instead."

"Yeah, I'm down for somewhere warm… like that place you were telling me about, the beautiful island. Gordo or something like that. How about we head there?"

Beckett cringed. After what had happened in the Virgin Gorda, he wasn't sure he'd ever be able to show his face in the Caribbean again.

"No, I'm partial to the Carolinas—South, to be exact. Ever since I was a boy, I always wanted to go to South Carolina. There's just something about their beautiful accents, their—"

"Bullshit," Suzan muttered. "Pure bullshit."

"No, it's true," Beckett joked as he placed the final plate in the drying rack. "My entire life, I only just wanted to see—"

"Redneck hillbillies?" Suzan finished for him, a scowl on her full lips.

"Don't be racist, Suzan. It's not becoming of you." Suzan sighed, but Beckett ignored her. "Just look at that headline: *Father Alister Cameron Cures Death*. I just *need* to go there. For science. For medicine. I mean, he *cures* death, Suzan. What kind of doctor am I—will you be—if you don't investigate the good man's claim. What kind of *humans* would we be?"

Suzan rolled her eyes, but he could tell that she was cracking.

"You're not going to embarrass me, are you?" she asked, tracing a line over the Xs on the priest's face with her finger.

Beckett grinned.

"Of course not, lover. I wouldn't dare embarrass you."

Suzan's face twisted; she absolutely hated when he called her *lover*.

"Fine. But I want five—no six-star accommodations. Goddammit, I want to stay at the mayor's house."

"Oh, please, easy on the blasphemy," Beckett joked. "But you can have whatever you like, my love. But first… are you ready for tonight?"

Chapter 7

"THESE GUYS... THESE SEXUAL PREDATORS?" Dunbar
continued, his anger rising. "They don't just stop at six or
seven or ten. Once they start, they keep on getting more and
more sadistic."

Sgt. Yasiv took a drag of the cigarette and looked over at
his friend. Dunbar had joined him outside after PO Tully
Salzman had left, even though he didn't smoke.

"You seem to know a lot about these perverts."

"Yeah, well, one day I want to have kids. And the more
you know... you know how it is. Knowledge is power."

Yasiv took another drag. Clearly, his friend had put a lot of
thought into this.

"Do you want to be a sergeant, one day?" Yasiv asked,
eager to change the subject.

Dunbar scoffed.

"You kidding me? To go through the shit that you've been
through? No thanks. Not for me."

Yasiv couldn't help but smirk. The truth was, no one had
asked him if he wanted to be a sergeant. He was just thrust
into the position without so much as a meeting with HR.

*Here you go, here are the keys to 62nd precinct. You'll report to
the Deputy Inspector... oh, wait, that post is currently vacant. Then
you'll report to the mayor... naw, that won't work, either. Me then,
the DA. Talk to me. Now be a good lad and go about your business.*

"What, then?"

Dunbar didn't hesitate.

"SVU."

Yasiv was surprised; the first time they'd come across a
body together, Dunbar had to excuse himself to vomit. He
didn't hold it against the man, but the Special Victims Unit?

Sex crimes, often against children? That was some next-level shit.

And yet the man's passion was obvious.

"SVU, that's where I want to be."

Yasiv nodded.

"Well, I'll tell you what, Dunbar, I'll do what I can to get you where you want to go. But I'll be honest, I could use you here. Even after all the indictments, not all rats sank with the ship. And I can trust you, which is more than I can say about most others in our precinct, or any other."

He paused, waiting for Dunbar to fill in the silence.

The man didn't.

"SVU... okay, I get it. As you know, the DA is pressuring me to find Wayne Cravat, which fits in nicely with your plan. You want to join me on this one on a full-time basis?"

Dunbar nodded a little too enthusiastically.

"I've got some other cases on the go, but—"

"Pass them onto someone else. We need to focus on finding Wayne, and then we'll go from there. What do you say?"

Yasiv held his hand out. "Partners?"

Dunbar grinned and shook it.

"Partners. So, when do we get started?"

Sgt. Yasiv turned his eyes skyward. The sun had long since set and the stars were peeking through the clouds. Or maybe those were just the lights of New York City; they were indistinguishable, after all.

"Right now, that's when we start. Come on, get your gear. The faster we can find this guy, the less likely he is to take another victim."

Chapter 8

AFTER BECKETT FINISHED HIS SCOTCH, and Suzan was nearly done with her glass of red wine, he turned to her and yawned.

"I'm getting tired," he said. They were watching some nonsense on TV, a reality show that, in essence, pitted one dimwit against another for cash. It reminded him of something he'd seen on the Internet long ago. Some guy with too much money and not enough morality went around paying homeless people cash to fight each other. It was horribly tasteless, but it wasn't a stretch from what passed as quality programming these days.

"You're never tired, and you never sleep," Suzan shot back.

"Don't you have an exam tomorrow?"

Suzan nodded.

"Yeah, but I'm all tapped out. Besides, it's just an anatomy class and I can think of better ways of studying than reading a book. There's no substitute for hands-on learning."

Beckett smiled.

"Oh really? Then what's this?" He reached out and gently traced a line from behind her ear to her chin.

Suzan turned into him as he did this.

"Mandible," she said. Her voice was husky now and Beckett's grin grew into a full-fledged smile. He knew just how to get to her.

Beckett continued down her chin to the hollow of her throat, resting in the crevice between her collar bones.

"And this?"

"Jugular notch."

Lower now, to the top of her breast. She was wearing a thin T-shirt, and he could see her nipples harden beneath the fabric. He continued even lower and gently grazed her nipple with the pad of his thumb.

"Areola," Suzan whispered. Temptation suddenly overwhelmed her, and she knocked his hand away. Then she slung her leg over and straddled him. Before Beckett was even sure what was happening, Suzan was kissing him, hungrily probing his mouth with her tongue.

Her breath was coming in shallow gasps and Beckett felt the front of his jeans become tight.

He gently moved her away from him and pulled her T-shirt over her head, revealing her bare breasts. Her skin was covered with goose pimples and she shivered. Beckett cupped one of her breasts then leaned forward, gently rubbing his cheek against her nipple.

Then he let go, and she leaned back, looking down at him.

"Don't stop," she said quietly. "Why are you stopping?"

"Tell me that you're going to come with me to South Carolina," he teased. "Promise me."

Suzan rolled her eyes and then reached down between his legs. She grabbed his penis through his jeans and squeezed. *Hard.*

Beckett winced.

"Promise *me* that you won't embarrass me," she countered.

"I promise," Beckett said. And with that, he grabbed her breast again and gently flicked her nipple. Suddenly, her hand was no longer squeezing his penis, instead, she'd unzipped his fly and was trying to pull it through the opening.

Suzan used her free hand to encourage him to grab her other breast at the same time.

Beckett was forced to uncross his fingers before he obliged.

Chapter 9

"ACCORDING TO TULLY SALZMAN'S NOTES, this is where Wayne Cravat worked. *Lucius Meats.*" Dunbar pulled back from the sheet of paper and made a face.

"It sounds like a strip club," Yasiv remarked.

"No kidding," Dunbar said. "And he worked mostly in the sausage department, loading different meats and whatever else they put in the goddamn things in the grinder. Let me ask you something, Yasiv? Why do these assholes always have to have creepy jobs? Why can't they just do normal things? Like work in a bookstore or be a web designer?"

Yasiv thought about this for a minute as he stared out the window. Lucius Meats was a meat packing plant roughly fifty miles from 62nd precinct. It was a twenty-four-hour plant that provided meat for the grocery stores in the area as well as a handful of restaurants. Even now, as the hour approached ten at night, the lights were on, and there was a fair bit of activity on the docks. People smoking, others, like them, sitting in their cars.

"I think it's the other way around," Yasiv said. "I think it's the people that make the job creepy. Think about it, if Wayne Cravat was a postman, you'd think that that was a creepy profession."

"You might be right."

"You know why most child molesters are priests or teachers or security guards... that sort of thing?"

"Yeah, so that they can be close to their prey. It's not the job that made them that way, but the way they are that made them choose the job."

"Which makes me wonder why Wayne Cravat works at a meat factory," Yasiv said, as he opened the door and stepped into the night. "Come on, Dunbar, let's get in and out of here as fast as we can. It stinks."

***

"Yeah, I know Wayne. Hard to miss that guy. Not so flush in the brains department, if you know what I mean," the man said as he jabbed a pitchfork into a plastic-lined cardboard box full of pig parts. He skewered some meat, then dropped into a silver hopper.

The smell inside the factory was predictably worse, a gamy scent mixed with artificial lemon cleanser. It was making Yasiv's head spin.

"You mind stopping that for a second?"

The man sighed then placed the butt end of the pitchfork on the ground and turned to look at him. He'd seen some rough times, this man had. Even with the white lab coat splattered with blood, the dual hairnets, one on his head and one on his chin, it was clear that he'd led a qualified existence. It was also clear that he had developed a distrust for police officers.

"Thanks," Yasiv grumbled. "So why did you hire the man?"

He shrugged.

"Management told me to, that's why."

Yasiv had just about given up. He was getting nowhere fast with this man and considered leaving the plant entirely before Dunbar chimed in.

"Yeah, I could see how that would piss you off. You have kids—" Dunbar's eyes darted to the name tag on the man's blood-splattered coat— "Frank?"

"Yeah, two kids. Why?"

There was something in what little was visible of his face—just his eyes and nose—combined with the way he said those words that let Yasiv know that while he did have children, Frank likely hadn't seen them in a while. Divorced, most likely. Wife left with another man and took the kids.

"You know what Wayne did, right?"

"I heard rumors, everyone around here was talkin' about it. Don't like the news much, so I dunno for sure. Alls I know is that he kept to *hisself* before and after he was arrested."

Yasiv's ears perked.

"You mean Wayne worked here before he was arrested?"

Frank nodded.

"Yeah, started a month or two before. When he was arrested, the union stepped in and put him on leave or some bullshit, and he got his job back once he beat the case."

"And you're sure he hasn't been at work for the last three days?" Yasiv asked.

Frank shook his head.

"No, that's not what I said; I said that I haven't *seen* him in three days. You can check the timestamps, but I didn't work on Monday. I was in yesterday and today, and he ain't here. Was scheduled, though."

Yasiv looked over at Dunbar, who scribbled this information on a small pad.

"Any idea what this Wayne guy liked to do after work?"

"The fuck should I know? He ain't my friend."

Yasiv nodded. Even if they were pals, admitting to being cozy with an accused child molester and murderer wasn't something that you'd readily admit to.

"Look, I gotta get back to work. You want to talk to somebody, talk to the supervisor."

"I thought you were the supervisor."

Frank stared at him as if he had three heads.

"I'm the *night* shift supervisor. I'm talking about the supervisor, supervisor. Now can I please get back to work? I need this job."

In the way he'd said that last part was also revealing; the man was on parole, and this job was likely the only thing keeping him from being behind bars.

"Sure. Thanks for your help," Yasiv said, and then indicated for Dunbar to head back outside. Dunbar wasn't done yet, however; he pulled a business card from his pocket.

"Hey, man, all we want to do is catch this asshole. We hate him just as much as you do. If you hear anything around the shop, hear anything at all about where he might be, let us know, okay?"

The man begrudgingly took the card and jammed it into his lab coat pocket. Yasiv knew the likelihood of hearing from Frank ever again was next to nil. The man might hate child molesters as Dunbar might loathe them, but he hated cops more.

All ex-cons did.

Frank struck Yasiv as the type of person who liked to take care of problems himself, take matters into his own hands, and dole out justice as he saw fit.

Chapter 10

BECKETT STARED UP AT THE ceiling, his fingers interlaced and laid across his stomach. Suzan had fallen asleep more than an hour ago and was now snoring lightly at his side.

It was closing in on midnight—the witching hour—and for the life of him, Beckett couldn't find a way out of his current predicament. He had a fucking corpse in the basement, the corpse of a man *he'd* killed, the corpse of a child molester and murderer, who deserved everything he'd gotten.

And while Beckett wasn't unsettled about the body itself— he'd come across plenty of those during the course of both his professional and extracurricular activities—the prospect of it just sitting there, getting warm, the bacteria in the man's gut flourishing now that they were unencumbered by churning gastric juices, and the prospect of Suzan sleepwalking and discovering it, was enough to put him on edge.

The good news was that Suzan had agreed to go with him to South Carolina. He'd lied to her about why they were going there, of course; he harbored no childhood desire to see the area. Instead, Beckett had seen something in Rev. Alister Cameron's eyes, in both the newspaper photo and other images he'd managed to scour online, that drew him to the man like a magnet.

It was the same look he'd seen in Winston Trent's and Flo-Ann McEwing's eyes, and Donnie DiMarco's before that.

The Rev. may claim to have cured death, but Beckett was almost certain that he'd also caused it at one point in time, as well.

But a face-to-face meeting was required, just to be sure. And proof. He needed that, too. After all, what kind of harbinger of justice would he be if he just went around killing people because they had an off look in their eyes, telling as this might be?

No, Beckett had his code, and he would stick to it—he *had* to. He would reserve judgment for those who he was certain had committed murder, those who could not contain their urges and were destined to do it again.

And again. And again. Unless someone stopped them.

Shadows drifted across the ceiling as cars drove by outside. Their headlights squeezed through the vertical slats of the blinds covering the window, causing straight lines to form on the drywall above. These reminded him of his tattoo gun in the bedside table not three feet away.

He needed to add another tattoo to his collection, one to remind him of what he'd done to Wayne Cravat. He had eight now, one for each of his kills. One for each person who had either slipped through the hands of justice or who taunted her from just out of the good woman's grasp.

The tingling in his fingers had stopped, for the time being, at least. He found himself wondering, when he was alone and deep into a bottle of scotch, whether the tingling had always been there, or if he only noticed it after his chance encounter with Craig Sloan.

Beckett had relived that moment more than fifty times since it happened nearly two years ago. In fact, he chased it with every kill.

He'd been entrusted with the task of keeping the serial killer locked in his trunk, while Detective Damien Drake ran into the burning house to rescue Suzan. But Craig had shot his way out of the trunk and was heading down the side of the house. The man had almost slipped into the night when Beckett approached. He knew that Craig was out of bullets, but he also knew that if he just let the man walk, they might never find him again.

The first blow that he'd delivered with the palm-sized rock was only meant to incapacitate, of that, Beckett was certain. The seventh or eighth strike, however…

Beckett swallowed hard and turned to look at Suzan. She was curled on her side, her nose nestled close to his chest. The woman had been through a lot, and despite her sarcasm and tough outer shell, she was hurting.

Her father had been murdered by none other than the Skeleton King, or one of his many proxies—shot dead while serving a routine warrant. For a long time, she'd blamed her father's partner—Damien Drake—for his death. But that had come to pass when Drake himself started up a relationship with her mom, Jasmine. Shit, they'd even recently had a child together, making Suzan the older step-sister.

But as twisted as the soap opera of Suzan's life was, it was only the beginning. There were rumors, unfounded as they must be, that Jasmine herself was involved with the infamous ANGUIS Holdings Corporation. But rather than stick around and face these accusations head-on, the woman had opted to take her baby and flee.

No one had seen either of them in over a month.

Suzan loved to joke around, to talk, to shoot the shit. But rarely did she ever talk about herself, her own twisted life.

Beckett unfolded his fingers, reached over and brushed a lock of hair from her cheek.

He recalled something she'd said when the news of Winston Trent's suicide finally broke: *Looks like that asshole got what he deserved.*

She was wrong; Winston had deserved much worse.

"One day I'll tell you who I really am," he whispered. He hadn't meant to speak, and as soon as the words left his mouth, he felt silly.

Suzan stirred but didn't wake.

Beckett felt silly because there's no way he could tell anybody who he really was.

The only people who knew were those represented by the horizontal tattoos that started just below his armpit and continued down his ribcage.

Chapter 11

"HE CLAMMED UP PRETTY GOOD," Dunbar said as they made their way toward their car. Yasiv lit a cigarette.

"No kidding. He's not gonna talk to us."

"What about some of the other guys? Not a supervisor maybe but a fellow worker? You think they'd tell us where Wayne might be? Where he liked to go?"

Yasiv, cigarette dangling from between his lips, stared up at the moon.

"Probably not. Guys like him, like Wayne, usually stick to themselves. I doubt he had any friends at all, let alone at work. Like that Frank guy said, he was none too popular here. I'm surprised that they didn't make it so miserable for him that he had no choice but to quit."

"You think that happened? Maybe one of the guys got pissed off one day and took his anger out on Wayne? Did more than make him just quit?" Dunbar asked.

Yasiv thought about it. It wasn't out of the question. There'd been many a case of vigilante justice, especially when it came to accused child molesters.

"Maybe. We should follow up on Will's parents, see what they were up to the last few nights."

"I'd... I'd rather not. I mean, they've been through so much..." Dunbar let his sentence trail off. He was taking this personally, which was not conducive to a thorough investigation. Yasiv wondered what Dunbar would do if it came to light that Will Kingston's parents had something to do with Wayne's disappearance.

Yasiv knew what he would do, but he wasn't so sure about his partner.

"We gotta be level-headed about this, Dunbar. We can't—"

"Excuse me? Excuse me?"

Yasiv turned to see a man in a white lab coat hurrying toward them. Perhaps it was the fact that it was late at night, or maybe it was because the man was holding some sort of hook in his hand, but for some reason, Yasiv's hand immediately went to his gun.

"Can we help you?" Dunbar asked, taking a defensive stance.

The man stopped maybe a dozen feet from them, and then put his hands on his knees to catch his breath. He must have only just now noticed the hook in his hand, as he slipped it into his pocket.

"Who are you?" Dunbar demanded. The man finally caught his breath, stood up straight and offered his hand.

Dunbar glanced at the blood on the man's sleeve and opted not to touch him.

"Sorry," the man grumbled, pulling his hand back. "My name's Kyle, Kyle Hill. I work here at the plant, for a long time, actually. I heard you guys in there talking to Frank, asking about Wayne."

Out of the corner of his eye, Yasiv saw Dunbar clench his jaw, and decided that it might be best if he stepped in.

"Yeah, we want to talk to Wayne, that's all," he offered, trying to keep things light. "You know where we might find him?"

The man rubbed the back of his neck, looking off to one side as he spoke.

"Nah, I don't—"

"Before you lie to us, keep in mind that you're protecting a man who was accused of raping and murdering a boy—an eight-year-old boy," Dunbar said, standing up tall, and puffing out his chest.

The man, who had been averting his eyes, suddenly looked at Dunbar.

"No, not Wayne. He didn't—he didn't do that."

"Just because some asshole on the jury couldn't make up his mind, doesn't mean he didn't do it," Dunbar shot back. "I saw the video. Everyone did. I *know* he did it."

Yasiv raised an eyebrow; he didn't know what video Dunbar was referring to. Clearly, not *everyone* had seen it.

"Think whatever you want, man, but trust me on this one. Wayne didn't do that. He didn't do nothin'."

Dunbar stepped forward aggressively.

"Yeah? And why are you so sure, huh?"

Yasiv flicked his cigarette and it erupted into sparks.

"C'mon, Dunbar. Let's get out of here."

Dunbar stared the man down for a moment longer, before turning to head to the car. But, apparently, Kyle wasn't done yet. He reached out grabbed for the back of Dunbar's arm. The detective spun around, while at the same time, grabbing the man's thumb. He twisted, immediately bringing Kyle to his knees.

He cried out, but Dunbar held fast.

"Don't touch me. Don't you *ever* touch me."

Yasiv immediately kicked into action, cursing himself for letting it go this far.

"Dunbar, let him go."

Dunbar glowered at the wincing man.

"Don't you ever fucking touch me."

"Dunbar..."

Dunbar let go and held his hands up while taking a step backward.

"You saw him, he tried to grab *me*."

"Yeah, yeah, I saw," Yasiv said, readying himself for another outburst.

The entire encounter was out of character for the big detective. He wasn't usually aggressive in the least.

What the hell is going on here?

"Go back inside," Yasiv ordered. The man looked at him with wide eyes, and then rose to his feet. He turned and took a handful of steps before stopping. Yasiv shook his head. "Just go—"

"Harvey Park Church in Queens. Every night at ten."

Dunbar sneered.

"What'd you say?"

Kyle cleared his throat and repeated the words. And then, before either of them could question him further, he started running back toward the meat factory.

"What the hell was that?" Dunbar asked when the man was out of earshot.

Leaning on the hood of his car, Yasiv looked over at his partner and shrugged.

"I dunno… maybe he thinks you need salvation. Shit, you need *something*."

Chapter 12

BLOOD FLOODED BECKETT'S NOSE AND mouth like an ebbing tide. In addition to not being able to breathe, he also gagged; the fluid had a strong metallic taste that churned his stomach. He flailed, but the sea of blood kept dragging him down.

His eyes snapped open, but at first, all he saw was red.

"I didn't do it!" he heard someone shout. Wayne Cravat's pale face suddenly came into focus, hovering over him. "I didn't do it!"

The words weren't coming from his mouth. Instead, the man seemed to breathe them through the gash in his throat.

Wayne's entire body suddenly materialized, and all his substantial weight was pushing down on Beckett. Blood was flowing out of his neck relentlessly, unbidden, unrepentant.

Beckett was in full survival mode now, desperately trying to clear the geyser of fluid from his face.

"I didn't do it!" Wayne screamed again. The way the words were whistling out of his neck wound was horrible. "*I didn't do it!*"

Somewhere in the distance, he heard police sirens.

Beckett tried to look around, to figure out where he was, to find a way out of this nightmare. But Wayne had other ideas. The man suddenly leaned down close, bringing the flapping and wheezing scalpel incision within inches of Beckett's face. Blood continued to flow from the orifice, but the words that accompanied the deluge were somehow clear.

"I didn't do it."

The makeshift mouth was so close that Beckett could feel the hot air that accompanied those words.

With a growl, Beckett finally managed to pull his hands free of the tar-like blood and he gripped the man's throat.

"Beckett! Beckett, wake up!"

Beckett blinked, and then immediately let go of Suzan's neck.

"What? What happened?"

He could still hear sirens and was unsure of whether this was a remnant of his dream or if the cops were after him. If they'd figured out what he'd done, who he'd killed, what he *was*.

"Christ, you squeezed me hard, Beckett."

Beckett wiped the drool from his cheek and tried to usher his mind back into reality.

The damn sirens…

He sat bolt upright, his eyes moving to the window, expecting to see the telltale sign of flashing lights.

"Is that the cops?"

Still massaging her throat, Suzan looked at him with her brow knitted.

"What the hell are you talking about? It's the alarm, Beckett. It's just the alarm."

All the air left Beckett's lungs then, and he grabbed his cell phone from the table and turned off the alarm.

Drawing a full breath, he observed the wreck he'd made of his bed. His sheets were a tangled mess, heavy with his sweat. Beckett realized that the breathing he'd felt—*Wayne's horrible, sputtering, gasping neck wound*—must have been Suzan.

"Jesus," he groaned, shaking his foot free of the bedsheets. "I'm sorry, Suzan. I was having a nightmare."

"No kidding," she said, still massaging her throat. "You kept saying that you didn't do it. And then you just grabbed me."

Beckett sat up and gently pulled her hands away from her throat.

"Here, let me see."

Her fair skin was red, but it didn't look like he'd bruised her or done any real damage.

"I think you'll be all right. Ice will help..."

Suzan looked unimpressed.

I was shouting that I didn't do it? Get it together, Beckett.

"I'm sorry."

"Ah, it's okay," Suzan replied, swinging her legs over the side of the bed and rising to her feet. She was wearing a long T-shirt and nothing underneath. As she moved, Beckett could see the bottom cleft beneath her ass cheeks and, despite everything, he felt a stirring in his sweat-drenched boxers.

Fuck off, Little Beckett. Not now.

"I'm really sorry. I don't know what happened. Must've drunk too much."

"Or you're overcome by guilt," Suzan said absently as she made her way to the bathroom.

Beckett could've sworn that she intentionally took a large step so that he could glimpse more of what lay beneath her nightshirt.

"I can... I can make it up to you?"

"Don't even think about it," she said as she started to brush her teeth. "Besides, don't you have that thing with the residents today? That special project you've been gabbing about all year?"

Beckett stared at Suzan as she moved her toothbrush up and down, side to side, which caused her breasts to jiggle seductively.

"Special project?"

Suzan pulled the toothbrush from her mouth.

"Yeah, some mystery box thing? You asked me to help, remember, but I can't because of my anatomy test."

Beckett sat bolt upright and he checked the time on his phone.

Seven forty-seven.

"Shit!" he cried as he pushed by Suzan and turned on the shower. "Shit! Shit! Shit!"

"What?"

"I'm going to be late, that's what!"

***

"You're okay to lock up?" Beckett asked as he grabbed his travel mug full of coffee and headed towards the door.

"Suzan? You gonna lock up?"

"Yeah, I'll see you tonight, okay?" Suzan hollered from the upper floor.

Beckett slipped his keyring off the hook and then opened the door.

"Thanks! Good luck on your test!"

He was about to step outside when his eyes fell on the basement door. It was closed, and since Suzan had been staying with him off and on for the past few months, as far as he knew, she'd never gone down there. It unnerved him to know there was a corpse in his basement, but he couldn't do anything about it—not today. Any other day he might've been able to call in sick, wait for Suzan to leave then deal with Wayne Cravat, but not today.

Suzan was right, he'd been planning this day for months, and she wasn't the only one he'd talked to about it.

If he missed today, people would notice. And that's the last thing he wanted. Things had finally started to settle down after the whole random organ fiasco; drawing attention to himself now was a recipe for disaster.

"I'll see you later," he whispered, his eyes locked on the basement door. Then Beckett left his home, all the while wondering why Wayne of all people haunted his dreams when none of his other victims ever had.

Chapter 13

THEY DROVE IN SILENCE FOR some time, heading away from Lucius Meats and toward the address that Wayne Cravat had listed on his parole form. The same address that PO Salzman claimed to have seen food cooking on the stove when he'd dropped by after Wayne had missed his first scheduled visit.

Yasiv debated bringing up how Dunbar had snapped, but he didn't think the man's action warranted any sort of reprimand. After all, Kyle *had* reached for him first.

Sure, Dunbar's reaction had been severe, but Wayne wasn't your normal parolee. And cases like his almost always caused those involved to overreact—it was expected. Yasiv's job was just to make sure that nobody stepped over the line.

"Dunbar?" Yasiv said, breaking the silence. "What video were you talking about back there?"

"Huh?"

Dunbar clearly still hadn't let go of the anger that brewed inside him.

"I asked what video you and that guy Frank were talking about back there. Something about Wayne and his trial?"

"Oh yeah," Dunbar replied, in a faraway voice. "Someone uploaded footage of Wayne, which led to his arrest. It showed him walking in the woods and he just 'happened' to find first Will's backpack and then his corpse. The prosecution said that it was some sort of trophy video, but the defense claimed that Wayne was only guilty of discovering the kid's body. Jury couldn't decide which was the truth, I guess."

"And the video is still online? You've seen it?"

"It was taken down, but it pops up every couple of weeks. I've seen it. Fucking creep smiles at the end like he knows he's gonna get away with it. Makes me sick just thinking about it."

Yasiv made a face. He'd seen enough death close-up, he didn't need it in video form as well. He took another left, moving away from the city center toward the outskirts.

Something occurred to him then; they'd been talking about Wayne's parole for some time now, and yet Yasiv didn't even know what the man was on parole for. He posed the question to Dunbar.

"Wayne may have been acquitted for killing Will, but he was convicted of concealing or improperly disposing of a body. Yeah, bullshit, I know. But still, they had to get him for something when that video leaked."

Yasiv internalized this and they drove in silence for several minutes. Eventually, he spoke up again.

"Hey, Dunbar? Can I ask you something?"

Now that his partner had calmed down considerably, he thought it safe to ask the question that had been on his mind ever since Lucius Meats.

"Yeah?"

"Why'd you go off back there? Why'd you get so pissed off?"

Dunbar scowled.

"That kind of shit... crimes against kids, it just gets to me. That and the fact that somehow guys like Wayne Cravat and Winston Trent, the worst kind of criminals, always seem to buck the system. It's like people don't want to believe that someone can be that bad, you know? That people are capable of the worst things imaginable."

Yasiv had a feeling that there was more to it than that, but he decided not to press. If Dunbar wanted to talk about it more later, he'd make himself available, but he wouldn't pry. They all had their secrets, and some were never meant to be told.

"Yeah, well, I guess I'm just jaded. I've seen the worst in people, and then some."

Yasiv took a hard right into the Happy Valley Trailer Park. He wasn't sure if the person who had named the place had a wry sense of humor or if the Park had just seen better days.

The single dirt road leading into the complex ran beneath a sign that was so weathered that it was impossible to read the name. On either side of the ad hoc road were rows of trailers one cockroach from condemnation.

"Shit, people live here?" Dunbar said under his breath.

"Yeah, and I think that one is Wayne's," Yasiv replied, pointing toward a white trailer with the numbers '212' taped to the side.

Yasiv pulled onto the grass in front of the trailer and inspected it through the windshield. It was actually in better shape than most of the places they'd passed on the way in. Sure, the siding was peeling in several places, but all of the windows appeared intact and the steps leading up to the door weren't rotted through completely.

"Yeah," Dunbar confirmed. "Two-twelve, this is it."

Yasiv checked his gun in his holster, but before getting out of the car, he turned to Dunbar.

"I'm taking the lead, all right? We're just here to have a look around and if we see Wayne, we just want to talk to him."

Dunbar nodded, but Yasiv made sure to hold the stare a little longer than was comfortable to make sure that his partner caught his meaning. The DA wanted Wayne back behind bars; what he didn't want was a complicated legal battle as the result of an unarmed man on parole being gunned down by an NYPD Detective.

"Yeah. I'll be okay."

Yasiv stepped from the vehicle and as soon as the cool air struck his face, the urge to smoke became nearly unbearable. He had to keep moving, keep occupied, otherwise nicotine withdrawal would set in, then he'd be the one with the itchy trigger finger.

The lights in the trailer were off and the grass leading up to the small wooden steps was straight and unbent. Yasiv aimed his flashlight on the grass and indicated the unmolested area with a flick of his wrist. Dunbar acknowledged the movement then raised his own light to the door.

"Doesn't look like anybody's been here for a while," he said, stating the obvious. As if confirming this point, there were several letters hanging halfway out of the outer screen door. "I say we knock, then see if the super can open it up for us."

As he spoke, Dunbar started forward, but Yasiv held his hand in front of the man.

"I'll go," he said, moving toward the steps. "And I don't know if we can go in. I don't know if PC covers—"

A light flicked on in the trailer, and Yasiv fell silent. The blinds in one of the windows spread and a dark set of eyes peered out.

"Shit, that's him!" Dunbar shouted. "That's Wayne!"

The man was already running for the door, his gun drawn.

Yasiv pulled his own gun from his holster and then the light flicked off.

"Dunbar!" Yasiv yelled. "Dunbar, wait up!"

But Dunbar was beyond the point of no return. The detective yanked the screen door open, then tried the knob. The inner door was locked. With a curse, he reared back and planted his boot right next to the dented doorknob. The wood

was so saturated with moisture that it flexed in the frame but
didn't break.

"Dunbar!" Yasiv shouted. He was on the bottom step when
he heard another door opening, followed by an earthy thump.

As Dunbar drew his foot back again, Yasiv focused on the
sound and realized that he could now hear footsteps moving
away from them.

"Dunbar! Dunbar, he's out back! He went out the back
way!"

Without waiting for his partner to reply, Yasiv turned and
bolted around the other side of the trailer.

He immediately spotted a shadow weaving in and out of
the rows of dilapidated trailers.

Yasiv pressed his flashlight to the bottom of his gun barrel
and took aim.

"NYPD! Stop! NYPD, stop, or I'll shoot!"

Chapter 14

"NO CHEATING. IF I CATCH you peeking under your blindfold, you will immediately be expelled, and I will seek criminal prosecution," Beckett proclaimed. For emphasis, he tapped his pointing stick against the chalkboard. Only it wasn't a chalkboard, but a Smart Board and it made a strange sonic sound. He cringed and quickly walked toward his six residents. "Do you understand?"

A grumble of something that passed as an affirmative spread through their ranks.

"This game is called the mystery—" Beckett paused. "—no, no, not *mystery*. It's called the *Bird Box* Medical Challenge. Yeah, I'm pretty sure it's copyrighted, but I don't care. That's what it's called, and these are the rules: rule number one, no talking about the Bird Box Medical Challenge to anyone, and in particular any IP lawyers. Rule number two: you do not talk about the Bird Box Medical Challenge to anyone. Rule number three: no peeking… shit, I already said that. Okay, this is even annoying me. Let's just cut to the Chase Adams: in the box in front of each of you, there is a body part. Men, the person to your left is your partner. They also have a body part in their box. Each pair of body parts is from the same person. Your goal is to first identify the body part—easy peasy. You can talk to your partner, but *no taking off your blindfolds. Capiche?*"

"Excuse me, Dr. Campbell, sir?"

Beckett rolled his eyes.

How can there be a question already?

He walked over to Maria and rapped his stick on the desk in front of her. She jumped.

"I'm not sure how you can have a question now, given that the instructions are clear and explicit and that you haven't started yet. But, by all means, go ahead and ask away."

The woman cleared her throat and started to tilt her head backward. Beckett pressed the stick to the top of her head to stop her, so she couldn't peek.

"I don't seem to have any gloves? I just—"

Beckett whacked the desk with his stick.

"No gloves! No gloves!" he shouted. "Just kidding, there are gloves on the desk. Slip them on, we're not spreading diseases here. Speaking of which, after you confirm the body part, I want you to identify the disease that killed the patient. That, my doting students, is the Bird Box Medical Challenge."

With that, Beckett took a step back and surveyed his residents.

The six remaining doctors had been with him for more than half a year now, and he was actually impressed with both their aptitude and their ability to put up with his unorthodox teaching methods. Predictably, they were led by Grant McEwing, better known as Boy Wonder or Doogie Howser or Dr. Gregory House, who seemed to know everything.

Except for who really killed his sister, that is.

Beckett massaged the tattoos under his arm. He was impressed not just by the man's didactic memory, but also by his ability to deal with the diarrhea storm life had thrown his way. First, his father dies of cancer, then his sister goes off the rails and starts killing people, then she meets her unfortunate end at the hands of Yours Truly.

Grant may be socially awkward, but he was also brilliant and trustworthy. If circumstances had been different, he might even consider the man a friend.

Beckett shook his head and went back to his desk to observe the hilarity at a safe distance. The first challenge was to put on gloves while blindfolded, which was no easy task, especially considering that Beckett had made sure to give each resident gloves one size smaller than they were used to.

Eventually, however, they managed and then hesitantly reached into their mystery boxes.

I should try this on Halloween, he thought. *That would be a real treat. Or trick. Ha, you're hilarious, Beckett.*

"Take your time, people, you've got an hour. Use it. Feel your organ, caress it, *love* it."

Beckett got his phone out and set a timer for thirty minutes.

Grant was the first to start, of course. He started to massage the diseased liver in a way that made Beckett shudder.

Okay, yeah, I'm not going to watch this.

Instead, he pulled out his phone and started doing a little more research on Rev. Alister Cameron's impossible claims.

"Curing death, *phff,*" he whispered to himself as he read. Most of the articles consisted of the Reverend's braggadocio or anecdotal claims of his super mega powers. But there was a line at the end of the article in the Times that caught his attention: *In addition to testimonials, genetic testing confirms that several parishioners of Rev. Alister Cameron's parish have been cured of a rare, hereditary version of Creutzfeldt-Jakob disease and cystic fibrosis, among others.*

This couldn't be true, of course. Neither disease was 'curable'; they were both fatal genetic conditions.

"I'm done."

Beckett wasn't surprised to see that it was Grant who made this proclamation.

"Fine, recite the alphabet backward, then. As for the rest of you, you've got ten more minutes."

Chapter 15

THANKFULLY, YASIV DIDN'T HAVE TO shoot the man from the trailer. In truth, he wasn't sure that he would have, given that it was unclear if it was even Wayne, or if he had just cause.

"Please, don't shoot!" the man shouted as he put on the brakes and raised his hands. "Please, don't shoot me!"

"Keep your hands up and drop to your knees," Yasiv instructed as he moved toward the man. A red-faced Dunbar suddenly appeared at the sergeant's side and, knowing how amped up the detective was, Yasiv purposefully stepped in front of him as he approached the man on his knees.

"Now, I want you to slowly interlace your fingers and place them on the back of your head. *Slowly.*"

Again, the man obliged.

"All right, no sudden—*dammit!*"

Dunbar pushed by him and grabbed the man by the wrist and pulled him backward. He cried out as he folded onto his own heels before his feet shot out in front of him.

"You're going back to prison, you piece of shit," Dunbar swore as he started to drag the man across the patchy lawn.

"What? What'd I do? What the fuck'd I do?"

Yasiv tucked his gun into his holster and shined the light on his partner.

"Let go of him, Dunbar."

But Dunbar was so incensed that it wasn't clear he could hear anything but his own voice. He just continued to curse.

What in the hell is wrong with him?

Yasiv shined the light directly in Dunbar's face, which finally got his attention. He let go of the man's wrist and took a step back.

The commotion had drawn people out of their trailers, some of whom were aiming cell phones in their direction.

"Keep it together, Dunbar."

"It's not him," Dunbar growled. "Yasiv, it's not him."

Before Yasiv could flick his flashlight in the direction of the man on the ground, a burly man brandishing a baseball bat stepped from the doorway of his trailer.

"Hey, what's going on over there?"

Yasiv pulled out his badge and flashed it in the newcomer's direction.

"NYPD, go back inside."

This failed to dissuade the man. He actually took a step forward and adjusted his grip on his bat. Yasiv frowned and deliberately placed his free hand on the butt of his gun.

"I said, go back inside."

The man growled and cursed under his breath but did as he was ordered. Only then did Yasiv turned back to Dunbar.

"What do you mean it's not him?"

"It's not Wayne Cravat," Dunbar said angrily. "Fuck, I don't know who this clown is, but it's not Wayne."

"I'm—I'm reporting you guys. You assaulted me, man. I got rights, I-I-I—"

"Shut up," Yasiv warned. "Dunbar, you sure it's not—"

"I'll sue, I'll sue the entire NYPD. This maniac just broke my knee or some shit, everyone here saw that. They saw—"

"I said shut up. Dunbar, cuff him."

"Cuff me? Why—"

Dunbar strode forward and teased his handcuffs from his belt. Then he roughly grabbed the man's arms and twisted them behind his back. He cried out again, but his bravado was suddenly nowhere to be found. Nor were his threats of legal action.

"Why? *Why*? Because you were breaking into a known child murderer's trailer, that's why. Now get the fuck up. You're coming back to the station with us."

Chapter 16

"YOU DONE? YEAH, YOU'RE ALL done. Pencils in the air and step away from your culinary creation."

Despite the inanity of the comment, all the residents moved away from their boxes.

"Can we take our blindfolds off?" Maria asked.

"Of course not. Now, there are six of you so—carry the one—that means there are three different diseases. Let's start with… I'll just pick at random… Maria, let's start with you. Please tell me what the organs you felt were, and what disease they were afflicted with. Trevor or Taylor or whatever the hell your name is, you can help her when she struggles."

"Well… my first organ was definitely a heart and the second was a brain. Part of the brain seemed to have some bleeding or an abscess or something in the pre-frontal cortex, while the heart was covered in fat. I think… I think my patient died of an aneurysm due to being obese, which led to the fatal heart attack."

"Why would you think that the person had the aneurysm first, which led to the heart attack, and not the other way around?" Beckett asked, tapping his stick on the desk as he spoke.

"I mean, it's just because I think that, umm, I guess—"

Beckett whacked the desk hard and the woman jumped.

"Right, so let's not do any guessing. This isn't the Price is Right. And Trevor? Shame on you for watching the poor girl suffer. I assume that you concur with her assessment of the aneurysm and the heart attack?"

"I do," the man with the manbun confirmed. "I would say that the aneurysm occurred first, due to the radius of bleeding. If the patient had the heart attack first, it would be unlikely to produce that much bleeding in the brain."

"Very good. I see that you're more than just a man with pretty hair," Beckett remarked. "But that was the easy one. All right, moving on, Pedro and Margo? What were your organs and what disease did your unfortunate patient suffer from?"

Pedro or Pablo—Beckett was horrible with names—took center stage.

"We had an eyeball and some sort of bone," he stated with confidence. Almost immediately, Margo contradicted him.

"No, that's not right, it wasn't an eyeball—"

Beckett tried to keep a straight face, but he couldn't. He broke out into laughter.

"Don't be coy with me, Pedro. An eyeball? *Please.* Don't act like you've never played with your balls before. Margo, I see you have more experience than your partner. Why don't you go ahead and learn him *something*?"

The girl cleared her throat and shifted in place uncomfortably. Beckett hadn't intended on his residents keeping their blindfolds on the entire time, but this was turning out to be very amusing.

"We had a testicle with a tumor. The bone was brittle around the head, so I'm thinking that the person died from testicular cancer that spread to the bones? Most likely—"

"Okay, that's enough, Margo," Beckett said, with a chuckle. "No more talk about balls and head, I don't have enough street cred to survive another #metoo allegation. But, for the record, you are correct. Okay," Beckett said clapping his hands together. "Now onto you, Boy Wonder and Bat Girl, you got the difficult one. Let's hear it."

There was no way that even Grant would get this one correct; Beckett had deliberately chosen an exceedingly rare disease.

"We had two organs," Grant McEwing began, "a liver and an eyeball."

Pedro reached up and started to lift his blindfold but stopped when Beckett whacked his stick again.

"Pedro, hands down or the next one will be across your knuckles."

The man's hands dropped to his sides.

"Go on, Doogie."

Grant nodded.

"As I was saying, we had an eyeball and a liver. The liver was afflicted with diffuse nodules, which were primarily concentrated to the right lobe, but there were a few in the left. I suspect that these were metastatic nodules, based on their texture and multiplicity. The eyeball was stiffer than I expected, although it's difficult to tell if this was a consequence of processing or a result of increased intraocular pressure. However, due to the nature of the liver nodules, I suspect that the latter is correct. Therefore, based on these facts, our patient suffered from uveal melanoma, which metastasized to the liver. Our patient died from liver failure."

Beckett gaped.

No way. No fucking way.

"Am I correct?"

Beckett blinked several times and stared at the organs lying in the glass containers.

Oh, I really thought I was going to stump you this time. Fucking Doogie Howser.

"Shit, you're right. You cheated somehow, but you are correct. I hope you guys learned something today, other than the fact that Margo is a bit of a freak. You can tell a lot about organs and cause of death even if, for whatever reason, things aren't in their correct anatomical location or if they are occluded by some process."

Maria raised her hand and Beckett rolled his eyes.

"Yes? What is it now?"

"Can we take the blindfold off?"

Beckett whacked the desk.

"No! You must keep your blindfold on for the rest of the day. It is mandatory if you want to pass my class. Also, I'm going away for a week, but I have eyes everywhere. I expect you to keep up on your studies, go to bed no later than ten o'clock, and get plenty of exercise. Don't drink, don't do drugs, don't drive fast cars. Most importantly, don't fart in the tub."

"Where are you going?" Pablo asked.

Before Beckett could answer, Trevor chimed in.

"Prison?"

"Haha, very funny. No, I'm not going to prison, I'm going on vacation. Wait, scratch that, just in case the IRS is listening, I'm going on an ultra high-tech holistic vegan medical journey into my metaphysical penumbra. Huh, that sounded kinda sexy. Anyway, in all seriousness, you guys did great today. I'm proud of you, my children."

After a fake sob, Beckett hurried from the room, leaving his students standing in place with their blindfolds on.

I wonder how long it will take before they realize that I'm gone. I wonder—

"Beckett."

He whipped around and was shocked to see Suzan coming at him. She was smiling, a clear indication that she'd done well on her test.

She wasn't as smart as Grant—nobody was—but she was a seriously skilled medical student. She was destined for great things if being associated with Beckett didn't drag her down, that is.

Beckett stopped smiling the moment he saw the bags draped over her shoulders.

"This is a surprise," he said cautiously.

"Our flight leaves in an hour—let's get a move on."

He gulped.

"Uh, Suzan, I can't leave right now. I have to—"

Suzan threw a bag at him, which he barely managed to catch by sandwiching it against his chest. Then she tugged on his arm.

"I heard you in there... you can leave. Besides, this is non-negotiable, Beckett. You've been promising to take me on this vacation for months now, and this is the only way I can get you to go, I know it. The tickets have been bought—with your credit card, by the way—accommodations have been booked. We are going to South Carolina, *baby*."

Beckett chewed the inside of his lip.

How can I go? I've got a goddamn corpse in my basement.

"But I can't—"

Suzan suddenly stopped smiling.

"What's wrong? I packed your very best rock T-shirts. Even bought some of that hair gel you like to use. Come on, Beckett, don't be a buzzkill. Let's go on this vacation. You *owe* me. We *have* to go."

She batted her eyelashes at him dramatically, and he knew that there was no getting out of this.

Wayne Cravat would have to wait. After all, it wasn't like he was going anywhere.

PART II

The Lord Healeth...

Chapter 17

"YOU WANT A COFFEE OR something?" Yasiv asked as he
stepped into the interrogation room. The man with bushy
eyebrows and shaggy hair didn't even look up.

"No."

"A Coke? Anything?"

The man finally raised his eyes.

"What I want, is to go home," he whined.

Yasiv nodded and slid into the seat across from him. He
cast a quick glance at the two-way mirror and nodded.

"Well, you *can* go home, Brent; you can go home in an hour
or you can go home in two days. It's really up to you. You can
also have a lawyer any time you want, as per your rights that
my partner read you earlier. All you have to do is ask."

Brent's thin lips curled into a sneer.

"And let me guess, if I ask for a lawyer, I'll be here for two
days. And if I'm here for two days, I'll lose my job. If I lose my
job, I'll be thrown back in prison for violating my parole.
What's that called again? Catch something?"

"Twenty-two."

"What?"

Yasiv shook his head.

"Never mind. Look, I just want to know what you were doing at Wayne's place."

"I told you already, you and that guy who twisted my knee. Wayne's a friend of mine, and I was just checkin' to see how he was."

"A friend of yours… are you from the meat factory?"

Brent shook his head.

"No."

The abrupt reply gave Yasiv pause, but he decided to address it later.

"Okay, okay, so how long have you known Wayne Cravat for?"

Brent shrugged.

"About a year."

"And where did you guys meet?"

"We were introduced by a mutual friend at a fourth of July party."

Brent shifted in his metal chair as he answered this last question. The chairs in the interrogation room were designed to be uncomfortable, but it was clear that Yasiv's question had put him on edge. Another tell was the way he continued to ramble even after answering.

"Me 'n Wayne, we hit it off right away. Had a lot of things in common, I guess."

Yasiv could almost feel Dunbar's anger emanating through the glass. He decided to pick up the pace before the man came barging in and changed the entire tone of the interview.

"You know anyone else at that trailer park?"

Something dark passed over Brent's face.

"No. Nobody."

He was lying, Yasiv knew, but he let this slide.

"Okay, sure. Speaking of Wayne, when's the last time you saw him?"

"Three days ago. Wayne usually goes to the meetings at the church on Mondays, but he wa'nt there. I work nights but get Sunday and Monday off, so that's when I see him most weeks. When he didn't show up, I went by his place. That's when you and the other cop came. I wa'nt breakin' in or nothin', I was just visitin'."

"But then why when I showed up at the door, you ran out the back way?"

"Like I said, I'm on parole. I don't need to be gettin' involved with no cops."

Brent crossed his arms over his chest.

This guy thinks he's one slick bastard, Yasiv thought. He debated trying to trip him up, put him in his place, but decided against it. He would probe, poke tiny holes in the man's stories, but it was in Yasiv's favor for Brent to think that he had the upper hand.

That he was the smart one in the room.

"How did you know that it wasn't Wayne coming home?" The man shifted.

"Cuz. I seen you through the blinds, that's why."

Yasiv nodded and bit his tongue. He wanted to point out that Brent was also alone in Wayne's trailer with the lights off when he and Dunbar showed up, but that would only tip his hand.

"All right, all right. Why don't you tell me about these meetings, then. What are they about?"

Brent suddenly clammed up, pressing his lips defiantly and shaking his head.

Too easy to read, my friend. Way too easy.

"Brent, look, I know you don't want to be here—trust me, I don't want to be here either. But I also know that you want to keep your job, and I know that you want to help your friend. But if you don't—"

The man's eyes suddenly narrowed, and he glared at Yasiv.

"We don't talk about the meetings. They're private. I told you already, I don't know where Wayne is. I don't know what else I gotta say."

Yasiv leaned back in his chair and spun his pen across the webbing of his thumb.

"I know, I know. But I just want to help, too. I just need—"

Brent suddenly slumped back in his chair.

"I think—I think I want a lawyer."

Yasiv immediately rose to his feet and started toward the door.

"All right, Brent. I'll be right back; this interview's over."

***

"He's lying," Dunbar seethed, his eyes locked on Brent on the other side of the glass.

Yasiv nodded.

"Of course, he is; he thinks he's slick. See how he stopped talking the minute I asked about the meetings? What do you think they're about? AA? NA?"

Dunbar's eyes never left Brent, who was now shifting near constantly in his chair.

"More like child abusers anonymous," he hissed.

"Maybe. But Brent's only record is for shoplifting. Still, I think we should check out one of these meetings ourselves."

Dunbar made a face but remained silent.

"All right, I'm going to cut him loose," Yasiv said.

Dunbar finally tore his eyes away from Brent.

"You're *what*? You're going to let him go?"

Yasiv weighed his options.

"He's not going to tell us anything more. He—"

"But he was breaking into Wayne's trailer! Surely, we can keep him on that. Sweat him a little."

Now it was Yasiv's turn to observe the man in the interrogation room.

"We could, but that's not going to hold up. If we can't find Wayne, there's no way to confirm or deny that he wasn't just checking up on the man. He didn't steal anything, so at best the DA will probably just tack on a few months to his probation and leave it at that. And if the man is guilty of something more substantial, the minute he leaves the courthouse he's gone; we'll never see him again. If we cut him loose now, he'll think that he got the leg up on us. Maybe start running his mouth, get himself into trouble again."

Dunbar pointed aggressively at the glass.

"Yeah, or maybe he just leaves here tonight, breaks into someone's house and kidnaps a child."

Yasiv looked at Brent. He wasn't a clairvoyant; there was only so much information he could get from the short interview, and only marginally more during a long one. But Brent didn't strike Yasiv as somebody who was reckless. A reckless man would have more than one prior conviction for shoplifting. Dunbar might have fabricated this narrative in his head, but that's all it was: a fabrication.

"I'm going to cut him loose," Yasiv reiterated. It was clear that Dunbar wasn't happy about this, but the big man remained silent. "How about you gather all the stuff you can on the Will Kingston case in the meantime."

Dunbar's eyes widened.

"We're going to take the case?"

Yasiv shook his head.

"No, it's not our case to take. Our job is to find Wayne Cravat. But maybe there's something in there that can help us."

A small smile appeared on Dunbar's lips, and Yasiv shook his head.

This is not the way I want to spend my evenings, he thought glumly, as he opened the door and made his way over to Brent Hopper. *This is not the way I wanted to spend any of my time.*

Chapter 18

"Seriously? We've only been here for an hour and already you want to go to this church thing."

Beckett pressed his hands together in prayer and lowered his chin to his chest.

"When the Lord calleth, his minions musteth go visiteth," Beckett replied.

Suzan, who had been in good spirits up until this point despite the fact that their flight was delayed, and their rental car wasn't ready, wasn't having any of it.

"Beckett, come on, please. Let's go have a drink first, walk around, see the sights, shop, anything but go to the church."

Beckett's phone buzzed; it was a notification that Rev. Alister Cameron was due on stage in less than fifteen minutes.

"Suzan, we're gonna have plenty of fun on this vacation, promise. But this guy claims to have cured *death*… gimme a break! Let's go check it out, see what he has to say, *then* we'll go for drinks."

Suzan glared at him.

When she didn't say anything for several seconds, Beckett leaned in close with pursed lips. She predictably recoiled.

"You're not getting anything until we have that first drink."

Beckett grinned.

"Are you sure you can resist me for that long?"

Suzan turned and stormed out of the room, giving him the finger over her shoulder as she went.

Beckett chuckled, but the moment she was gone, he grew serious.

What the fuck are you doing here, Beckett? You've got a dead body at home more than seven hundred miles away. A dead body that is going to start to smell.

Thankfully, however, it was a cool fall in New York, and they were only scheduled to be in South Carolina for a week. A week was plenty to check out this nutjob Reverend, then head back home. They might even have time to make good on his promise to Suzan and have a little fun along the way.

Beckett threw on a fresh pair of jeans and a T-shirt and then messed up his hair. He was about to follow after Suzan when he spotted two items buried at the bottom of his bag: a silver flask and a black leather case. He took the latter out and opened it.

Did Suzan...

Beckett shook his head.

No, it was in there from my last trip, I just forgot to take it out. I think.

Beckett grabbed the flask next and opened it. It was empty, but his roaming eyes spotted a minibar in the corner of the room. He hurried over and cracked open three Crown Royal bottles and dumped them inside. He sloshed the liquid around a little then took a sip, just to make sure that nobody had tried to poison the queen.

After smacking his lips, he shoved the flask in his pocket and then started out of the room.

"Suzan, wait up! We must face our Savior together!"

***

Beckett nudged Suzan's leg, but she shooed him away with her hand without even looking at him. He nudged again, and this time she turned toward him.

"What? What do you want?"

Beckett didn't say anything. Instead, he just shook the flask down between his knees so that only she could see. As soon as Suzan's eyes fell on the silver exterior, they widened.

"Remember what you said about that first drink?"

Suzan reached out and forced his hand down under the pew.

"Not here, you idiot. We're in church. This is—"

"*Shh!*" a woman with a bouffant hairdo hissed at them, pressing a manicured finger to wrinkled lips.

Beckett made an 'o' face and then mock prayed two or three times before she looked away, shaking her head.

When he glanced back at Suzan, she was still glaring at him.

"Fine then," he whispered. "More for me."

Beckett somehow managed to unscrew the cap with one hand and then bent down low to take a sip. When he raised his head, he was surprised to see that Rev. Alister Cameron was now on stage, both hands held out to the heavens.

Oh God, look at this ass clown.

And look he did. So did everyone else; the place was packed, and Beckett and Suzan were lucky just to get a seat. There were at least a hundred people in the small church that had a capacity of maybe a third that many, most of whom were standing near the back wall. Beckett debated calling the cops or the fire department and reporting them, but a representative of both in full uniform was among the crowd.

Figures.

"My people, the Lord thanks you for coming here today. For those who are new, my name is Rev. Alister Cameron, and the Lord has bestowed me with a unique gift."

The crowd erupted into cheers, which caught Beckett by surprise. The man had literally just introduced himself and already people were slapping their palms together as if the man had just won the Super Bowl.

It's going to be like that, is it?

Beckett was likely one of the least experienced people at the service—both his parents had been agnostic—but this seemed, well, unique.

"Amen, amen," Rev. Cameron said, lowering his hands. The parishioners eventually followed his lead and fell silent.

Beckett glanced over at Suzan and was equally surprised that she seemed rapt by the man's words.

This is also... unique.

Although he couldn't recall ever specifically discussing religion with Suzan, he knew that she'd also been brought up in an agnostic household. There were rumors that her late father, Clay Cuthbert, had been involved with the Church of Liberation, but that was about as far from a religious organization as one could get.

Beckett shook his head and debated taking another drink, but quickly decided against it; this was too good to miss.

Rev. Cameron was smiling broadly, but the expression never quite reached his eyes... his cold, hard eyes.

Eyes like Ron Stransky's or Flo-Ann McEwing's.

"The gift that our Lord has blessed me with is an incredible one, as is what he told me: Death is but a disease, and I have the cure."

Chapter 19

"DETECTIVE CRUMLEY? MY NAME IS Sgt. Henry Yasiv from 62nd division, and this is Detective Steve Dunbar. You got a moment? I have a few questions I was hoping you might be able to clear up for me."

Yasiv hadn't been surprised to find Detective Bob Crumley still at work despite the late hour; he'd heard stories about the boys in SVU. They worked late, they partied hard, and they always got the job done.

The man spun around in his chair and simply observed Yasiv for a moment. He was eating a donut with one hand and had a coffee in the other. Yet, despite this cliché, he was rail thin, with thinning hair, a bushy mustache, and dark eyes set into pale flesh.

It looked like he hadn't slept in days, which was another thing that Yasiv had heard about the SVU boys.

"Yeah, sure thing. I'd shake your hand, but…"

Yasiv nodded.

"No problem. This is just a courtesy call, we're not here to take over your case, or anything like that."

Yasiv had learned early on that professional courtesy went a long way in the police force. He looked over at Dunbar, but the man kept mum; he was still pissed that they'd let Brent Hopper go.

Detective Crumley took a sip of his coffee.

"Sgt…"

"Yasiv."

"Sgt. Yasiv, we're dramatically understaffed here. And the first rule of SVU is that you gotta leave your fucking ego at the door. If you want to help with one of our cases, by all means. We could use it."

Yasiv was surprised. Usually, people got their back up when other departments started nosing around in their business. It looked like the SVU, or in the very least Detective Bob Crumley was a different breed entirely.

"Great... well, the DA has been putting pressure on us to find a man who skipped out on his parole officer. I'm thinking that you guys might know him? His name is Wayne Cravat." Something flashed over the detective's eyes, confirming that he was familiar with the man. "We just want to find him, put him back behind bars. I was hoping that you guys might have some more details about the places he likes to hang out, that sort of thing."

Another sip of coffee.

"Wayne Cravat... yeah, that was a clusterfuck of a case. The DA is on our ass now, trying to find a new suspect for Will Kingston's murder."

Yasiv made a face.

"Yeah, I don't suspect things will get any easier, either, until a new mayor is elected. But about Wayne, we went to his place of employment, Lucius Meats, and they say he hasn't been there for three days. We went to his house, still nothing."

"You went to Happy Valley? What a joke of a name, huh? Should be called Child Molester Paradise."

Yasiv raised an eyebrow.

"What do you mean?"

"Remember Winston Trent?"

Dunbar suddenly came to life.

"Yeah, murdered Bentley Thomas, but somehow beat the charge. He was so overcome by guilt that he'd killed himself. Good riddance, piece of shit."

Crumley raised an eyebrow.

"I'll admit, no great loss there. Not our finest moment, either; both men charged with molesting and murdering a young boy, both set free. Anyway, Winston lived in the same trailer park as Wayne Cravat."

Yasiv was taken aback by this; he must have missed it while going over the man's file.

"Really? Did they know each other?"

"Probably. We could never find a solid connection, but, you know, these guys tend to group together. If you've been to Happy Valley, then you've probably already seen that, met some of the local yokels."

Yasiv pictured the concerned resident coming out of his trailer brandishing a baseball bat.

"Pleasant bunch. So, if Wayne's not hanging out at the trailer park, where might he be?"

Detective Crumley took a bite of his donut, chewed twice, then swallowed.

"Either at the church or the bar. The devil or the angel, you decide which is which."

"You got an address for both?" Yasiv asked.

Crumley took another bite of his donut.

"The church is called Harvey Park in Queens on Chevy Chase Road, while the bar is a place called Local 75. It's in East Harlem, on Fifth, I believe."

"Thanks for your help, Detective Crumley," Yasiv said, extending his hand. This time, Crumley jammed what was left of the donut in his mouth and then shook it.

"No problem," he said with a spray of powdered sugar.

Yasiv turned to leave when Dunbar spoke up again.

"One more thing; you wouldn't happen to have a copy of the court proceedings for Winston or Wayne handy, would you?"

Crumley waved a hand toward the back wall indicating stacks of boxes.

"Twenty-one boxes. You're welcome to have at it."

Dunbar gaped.

"Really? And with all this, you still couldn't convict either of them?"

Yasiv cringed. The man was trying to help them out, and yet Dunbar seemed to be looking for a fight. Thankfully, Crumley didn't take the bait.

"It looks like a lot, but for Wayne, at least, there wasn't that much substance there. All we really had is that video. To be honest, I'm surprised that the DA went ahead with the case, but I guess they were getting pressured from someone above them. Not surprising, what with Winston Trent beating his charge. I think the DA was just hoping to wrap it up quick, take some of the attention away from the heroin smuggling fiasco."

There was really nothing in the man's words that Yasiv could find fault with. In addition to being helpful, Crumley also seemed level-headed and rational, two things that didn't often go hand-in-hand with being a police officer, SVU or otherwise.

"Yeah, I know how it is. Are you still investigating both cases?"

Crumley sucked his teeth.

"On the record? Sure. Off the record? Winston Trent killed that boy. As far as I'm concerned, that case is closed. As for Will Kingston, we're still looking into it, but the DA directed all our resources into Wayne Cravat. When that didn't pan out the way they'd hoped, we gotta start from scratch. It's a slog."

"I bet. Again, I—"

"Do you have the Coles Notes on the Wayne Cravat indictment?" Dunbar interrupted. Yasiv shot his partner a look, but Crumley was once again unfazed.

"I'll tell you what, I've got the notes that I initially gave the DA, pretty much sums up what we had on Wayne—'bout ten pages. You wait here, and I'll get it for you."

"Thanks, you have been a great help."

Detective Crumley started to walk away, but then he stopped.

"I don't know if Wayne Cravat killed Will Kingston, but if he broke his parole, then I hope you catch his ass and put him back in prison."

"Me too," Detective Dunbar growled. "Me too."

Chapter 20

"**WOULD EVERYONE PLEASE PUT THEIR** hands together and join me in welcoming Bethany Anne Guthrie to the stage."

Beckett watched as a woman who looked to be in her mid-forties was hoisted up next to Rev. Cameron by several of his aids.

Most everyone in the audience erupted into cheers, but Beckett refrained; he had no idea what they were clapping about and doubted they did either. But he wasn't surprised; he'd already suffered through a half hour of this nonsense in which people cheered when the Reverend so much as broke wind.

"Bethany Anne, please tell the crowd how old you are."

"Twenty-three. I'm twenty-three years old."

Jesus, you should stay out of the sun, sister.

"And will you please tell the crowd what you were diagnosed with just three short months ago?"

"Oh yes, do tell, Bethany Anne," Beckett grumbled. "Was it presbyopia? Or maybe traveler's diarrhea?"

Suzan hushed him, but she was grinning at the same time. This whole day was annoying, and Beckett was beginning to regret his decision to come to South Carolina in general. Rev. Alister Cameron was nothing more than a charlatan, a snake oil salesman. The only sinister thing going on here was separating these poor folks of the cash in their wallets.

But his eyes…

Beckett leaned over and took a sip from his flask.

"Three months ago, I was diagnosed with a very rare genetic condition. A condition called Werner Syndrome."

Beckett suddenly sat up straight.

What the hell? Benjamin fucking Button?

"Yes, that's right. And why don't you go ahead and tell everyone what this condition entails," Rev. Cameron encouraged.

"It's a genetic disorder that causes premature aging. Basically, I age three times as fast as everyone else."

"Yes, and, unfortunately, this aging comes with everything that you might expect: heart disease, dementia, osteoporosis. It truly is a disease that robs one of their adolescence and early adulthood."

Beckett was so shocked by the Reverend's words that his mouth swung open. He'd expected the man to ramble on about non-existent conditions like chronic Lyme disease or gluten intolerance. But Werner Syndrome? Werner Syndrome was an exceedingly rare condition. Not only that, but it appeared as if the Reverend knew what he was talking about. Minus the curing part, that is.

"He's done his homework, I'll give him that," Beckett muttered. This time he was hushed by the elderly woman with the big hair.

Beckett stuck out his tongue and she looked away.

"The prognosis was grim, to be sure," Rev. Cameron continued. "But please, share with us the good news."

"I'm healed," Bethany Anne said softly. Then she raised her eyes and seemed to glare directly at Beckett. "I'm healed!"

With this second proclamation, not only did the entire place erupt into applause, but people rocketed to their feet.

When Suzan also started to rise, Beckett resisted the urge to pull her back down.

"I've cured death! The Lord gave me the power to cure death!" Rev. Cameron's screams could be heard over the roaring cheers.

Soon, Beckett was the only one who remained seated. He couldn't even stand if he wanted to; he was suddenly feeling sick to his stomach.

And this is how Jim Jones got everyone to drink the Kool-Aid, he thought. And then, in an ironic gesture, he raised his flask in a toast to the man and took two hefty swallows.

Chapter 21

"WELL, I'M CLEARLY IN NEED of repenting, but I'd rather check out the bar first, if it's all the same to you," Yasiv said as he smoked. When the detective didn't reply, he turned to the man in the passenger seat. "Dunbar? You even listening to me?"

"Huh?" Dunbar pulled his head out of the file that Crumley had given him. "What?"

"I said, we're going to the bar first. That okay by you?"

"Yeah, yeah, that's fine. Sure."

"What's so interesting in there, anyway?"

"Did you know that Wayne Cravat was brought up in an orphanage? That they found him living with his drug-addicted uncle after his mother and father just abandoned him when he was six?"

Yasiv shook his head.

"I don't know anything about this Wayne Cravat guy, save the fact that he was accused and acquitted of raping and killing Will Kingston and that he missed out on two parole meetings."

Dunbar didn't even acknowledge the comment.

"Yeah, after being shipped off to an orphanage, it looks like he was picked on a lot. In and out of therapy."

Yasiv took a left and then checked the street signs to make sure they were still headed in the right direction.

"Doesn't justify what he did," he said absently.

"No, of course not," Dunbar shot back. "Get this, when Wayne was fifteen, he was convicted of molesting an eleven-year-old girl. Claims he was tormented by her, and when he lashed out, he accidentally tore off her shirt. Scratched her chest, that sort of thing. No one could corroborate his story.

When he was nineteen, he was caught masturbating outside the window of a seventeen-year-old girl."

Yasiv thought about this for a moment.

"That's it? Nothing with other boys? Nothing between the masturbating thing and Will Kingston's murder? How old is he now?"

"Thirty-one. There are no other charges listed here, but we know how these sexual predators are. They don't just stop, they escalate. The sicko's probably responsible for dozens of unsolved sexual crimes over the years."

Yasiv didn't necessarily agree. He was no profiler by any stretch, but the two crimes that Dunbar had just recounted didn't necessarily indicate a sexual predator. A confused, probably angry teenager perhaps, but not the next Ted Bundy. Besides, by all accounts, Wayne Cravat wasn't the sharpest knife in the drawer, and to go under the radar for more than twelve years with the sexual inclinations that Dunbar suggested?

Highly unlikely. Not impossible, but improbable.

"What evidence do they have on him for the Will Kingston murder, anyway?"

Dunbar flipped through the sheets of paper.

"Mainly, the tape that surfaced online of him finding the body. He couldn't explain what he was doing in the woods, given that he admitted to never being there before. And yet, he just happened to find the boy's body, even though it was off the trail and buried in leaves. There was also an eye witness who picked him out of a lineup, says he saw Wayne hanging around Will's elementary school the day before he went missing."

Yasiv took all this in but refrained from commenting. Dunbar's anger was clearly mounting again.

"Yeah, and they still acquitted him. What a fucking joke."
Dunbar slammed the folder closed and tossed it on the dash.

Yasiv let the man stew in silence until he found a parking spot out front of *Local 75*.

"Technically, we're off the clock, Dunbar," Yasiv said as he stepped out of the vehicle.

Dunbar nodded, catching his drift.

"Good," he replied, pressing his lips together firmly. "Because I could sure use a drink."

"So could I," Yasiv admitted. "So could I."

***

"You ever seen this man in here before?" Yasiv asked as the bartender returned with his drink. The man didn't even look at the photograph until Yasiv produced a badge and placed it on the counter. "Just want to know if you've seen him in here, that's all."

The bartender, a man with a handlebar mustache and tattoos on his neck, looked at the photo and then nodded.

"Yeah, I seen him. I seen him in here and on the news."

"When's the last time you saw him in here?

"He's usually here every Monday, sometimes on the weekend. Always orders the same shit. A vodka with Sprite."

In his periphery, Yasiv saw Dunbar scribble this down.

"And last Monday? Two days ago? Was he here?"

"No, he wasn't here Monday."

Yasiv looked around, focusing on the area behind the bar.

"Any security cameras in here?"

The bartender shook his head.

"Nope. Lots of cops come in here, though, I figure that's security enough."

Yasiv raised an eyebrow.

"Really? From what division?"

The bartender shrugged.

""No idea."

"Then how do you know they're cops?"

The bartender stared at Yasiv and made a face.

"I can tell," he said simply.

Fair enough.

"Last time this man was in here; did you notice anything different about him?"

"No, same. He just orders his drink and sits down. Keeps to himself. One time, somebody recognized him from the news and started giving him shit, he just up and left. Didn't want nothin' to do with that."

"You're kidding."

The man's serious expression said it all.

"Did the cops know who he was? What he was accused of?"

The bartender shook his head.

"No, probably not. Like I said, that guy kept to himself. Cops come here to get loaded, forget about work, not put in overtime, if you know what I mean."

Yasiv thanked the man and paid him, making sure to leave a considerable tip. Then he turned to Dunbar.

"You get all that?"

Dunbar sipped his beer.

"Yeah, I got it. Don't understand it, though. What the hell was he doing coming here?"

"Drinking Sprite and vodka, apparently."

They fell quiet for a few minutes and Yasiv's thoughts turned inward.

Something wasn't adding up. Why would an accused child molester and murderer go to a bar frequented by cops? *Local 75* wasn't exactly in Wayne's neighborhood; he had to go out of his way to come here. But why? Either the man was rubbing it in the NYPD's face that he beat the Will Kingston rap, or he was just too stupid to realize where he was. And if the former was the case, why run away? If a cop assaulted him here, why not videotape it and keep it as ammunition for the next time he was charged. Because if Wayne Cravat was a sexual predator as Dunbar claimed, there most definitely would be a next time… wouldn't there?

Yasiv finished his beer and was about to order another one when a hand came down on his shoulder.

He turned, surprised to see PO Tully Salzman looking down at him.

"Detective Yasiv, Detective Dunbar, I'm surprised to see you guys here."

"Likewise," Yasiv said, shaking the man's hand.

The bartender was right; apparently, this was the place for cops to grab a drink after work. But that still didn't answer the question of why Wayne Cravat would come here.

And why the hell the man would be drinking vodka and Sprite, of all things.

Chapter 22

"COME ON, BECKETT, LET'S GO back to the Airbnb, get changed, go for a nice dinner," Suzan pleaded. At times like this, she seemed like the mature one, and Beckett a whiny teenager.

"I don't think that you appreciate the magnitude of what has happened here, dear child," Beckett said in a thick British accent. "This man, this servant of God, has *curethed deatheth*. The power of the Lord has been bestowed upon this man. I must shake his hand and converse with such an impressive healer."

"Jesus Christ, Beckett. Please, don't embarrass me."

"Why? You think maybe you'll have to come back here to be healed by this master of the mystic arts? Are you afraid that I might piss his holiness off, and he will be unable to cure you of toxic shock syndrome?"

Suzan threw up her hands. Beckett knew that her patience was wearing thin, but he was unable to help himself.

She started to walk away from him, but Beckett couldn't let her go.

"Something's not right here, Suzan," he said, taking a serious tone for once. "Let me just talk to the man, then we'll go for dinner and drinks. Just stick by my side, please."

Suzan huffed and puffed, but eventually agreed. He could tell that while she was incredibly annoyed, she was also curious.

They had to wait, of course; everyone wanted to touch Rev. Cameron's hand like he was the Dalai Lama or some shit.

It took forty-five minutes before most everyone had cleared out of the church, leaving only a few stragglers—one of whom was the police officer.

Beckett took a deep breath and approached Rev. Alister Cameron.

"Child of the Lord, it's my pleasure to meet you," the man said. He was large, both in stature and in personality. He was six-foot four and two-hundred and twenty pounds, if Beckett was inclined to hazard a guess, with thick, meaty forearms and hands that matched. His hair was a sandy blond and he had crow's feet around his eyes, from the sun and not stress, most likely. Rev. Cameron was also younger than he appeared in photographs. But perhaps he hadn't stopped at curing the prematurely aged but aging in general.

"The pleasure is all mine," Beckett said with a grin. He held out his hands, palms up. "Should I bow and kiss the ring, Rev. Cameron?"

Suzan elbowed him in the ribs and he stood up straight.

"No need; I'm not some sort of Savior. I'm only a vessel, a conduit for our Lord."

"My apologies, Reverend. I'm just not used to being around someone with your... power."

The Reverend held his palms out to his side in a grand, sweeping gesture.

"I am but a servant of the Lord, as are you. Now, what might I be able to help you with?"

Beckett immediately raised his hand, showing off his nub of an index finger.

"I'm afraid I might have dipped this into the holy water as I stepped through the doors... can you... can you fix it? I mean my girlfriend really misses it, she—"

Another elbow, this one hard enough to make him cringe.

And yet Rev. Cameron seemed unfazed.

"Ah, a skeptic. That's fine, I do not hold it against you. I agree that what is happening here, what the Lord has done, is difficult to believe."

"Nigh impossible," Beckett corrected. "Werner Syndrome? You really cured that? Because you'd be the first."

The Reverend's eyes narrowed, and Beckett finally thought that he'd broken the man's facade. But then he realized his error; Alister Cameron wasn't angry or frustrated with him but was trying to understand him. To *read* him.

Yeah, this is a nut you won't be able to crack, my good man.

"Ah, I understand now, my good son. You are a doctor."

Beckett crossed himself.

"Guilty as charged."

"Now, I understand your skepticism. But let me assure you that I have the genetic tests to prove that Bethany Anne was once afflicted by Werner Syndrome, but is now healed."

Beckett recalled the last line of the article about the Reverend in the Times.

"Well then, you wouldn't mind if I were to take a look at said genetic tests, would you?"

He expected the man to say no, to come up with something about how the Lord worked in mysterious ways, but Rev. Cameron was full of surprises, it seemed.

"But of course. In fact, why don't you and your girlfriend join me and my wife for dinner tonight? I would be happy to share these tests with you then. After all, I was a doctor once, and I know how important it is to have evidence backing up extraordinary claims."

"I—uhh—I—uhh—I think—" Beckett gave up.

A doctor? This guy was a doctor? And he wants me to join him for dinner? I would rather stick a white-hot needle in my eye. Even if he could give me two more inches, I wouldn't—

A third elbow in the ribs, this one hard enough to leave a bruise.

"I don't—I mean—"

"We'd be happy to," Suzan said with a shit-eating grin. "We'd be more than happy to join you in prayer before the meal, as well. Isn't that right, Beckett?"

Beckett glared at his girlfriend. He came here to investigate this asshole, not to break bread with him.

He made a face and gave in. After all, Suzan had gotten him good.

"But of course. I'll be sure to bring the wafers and wine," Beckett grumbled.

Chapter 23

"I HEARD THAT HE CAME here, yeah. Never saw him myself, though," PO Salzman told both Yasiv and Dunbar. They'd migrated from the bar to a booth.

Yasiv realized that he liked Tully, and thought that even under different circumstances, they might still be in a bar like this one having a drink.

"And you don't think that was strange?" Dunbar asked.

"I've read Wayne's file; nothing about his life is ordinary. Even though I'm his PO, our interactions were limited. He really didn't say much. Like I told you guys earlier, Wayne isn't really working with a full deck, if you know what I mean."

"Yeah, but he was allowed to drink? Like, as a condition of his parole?"

Clearly, Dunbar was taking his conversation in another direction. Yasiv was trying to keep things cordial, friendly, civil, but Dunbar had other ideas.

"Nothin' against drinking. So long as he kept a steady job, stayed away from schools and that sort of shit, he was okay. I'm telling you, he was a good parolee until he disappeared."

Yasiv was tired and the alcohol was making him sleepy. The beer in his hand was to be his last, he decided. He just hoped that things didn't escalate before then.

"Good parolee? It sounds like you liked the man," Dunbar remarked sourly.

Fuck. Here it comes.

Salzman sighed and roughly put his drink down on the table. Then he turned his entire body to face Dunbar, who was seated beside him. Yasiv's muscles tensed as he prepared to step between the two of them in case things got physical.

"Look, I didn't hate the man, that much is true. Did he do some fucked up shit in the past? Yeah, he did. Reprehensible shit, shit I don't condone. But I got a tough gig, man. These cons come at me one of two ways: they either try to bribe me or they try to intimidate me. Wayne wasn't like that. He just went about his business, kept to himself, and checked in on time."

"Yeah, he tried to keep a low profile, so he could keep molesting little boys," Dunbar said, refusing to back down.

"He was acquitted of that, Detective Dunbar."

"Yeah, I know, and OJ was acquitted of killing his wife. That doesn't mean they didn't do it."

Tully suddenly rose to his feet and Dunbar practically leaped up to meet him. The latter had a good forty pounds and maybe three inches on the PO, but it appeared that only one of them had any desire to take this further.

"I'm tired, boys," Tully said. "Sorry I couldn't be of more help."

Yasiv had to physically move Dunbar out of the way so that Salzman could get by.

"You helped plenty," Yasiv said. "Thanks. We'll be in touch if we find anything."

Tully gave him a tired look and nodded. Then he left the bar. When he was gone, Yasiv turned to Dunbar.

"You gotta keep it together, Dunbar. Seriously. PO Salzman had nothing to do with this, he wasn't on the jury that acquitted Wayne. He's just the man's PO."

Dunbar lowered his gaze.

"Yeah, I know. It's just that this type of thing gets to me."

"No kidding. The fact is, though, all we gotta do is find this asshole. That's it. Get the DA off our backs for a while. You can't take this so personally… that's when mistakes are made."

"You think that's what happened here? Someone took this case too personally and decided that if the court couldn't deal with Wayne, that they'd take care of him on their own?"

The question surprised Yasiv, and he had to think about it for a moment. In the end, he resigned himself to just rubbing the back of his neck.

"How the hell should I know? All I know, is that we need to find him. That, and the fact that I'm beat. I'm heading home to get some sleep. Want me to drop you off?"

Dunbar shook his head.

"No, I think I'll hang around for a bit."

Yasiv cringed; he didn't like that idea one bit. But the man was off the clock and he had no authority to tell him differently.

"All right, I'll see you tomorrow. We'll pick this up then. And Dunbar?"

Dunbar raised his eyes.

"Yeah?"

"Don't do anything stupid. You want that SVU job? Then stick to the plan. I'm telling you this as a friend."

Dunbar said nothing, which made Yasiv worry even more.

Chapter 24

"I THINK I HATE YOU, SUZAN Cuthbert," Beckett said.

Suzan laughed.

"You wanted this, not me. Shit, I wanted to go to Montréal. But no, you had to come here to check out some douchebag who claims to be able to cure death. This is your doing, Beckett, not mine."

Beckett rolled his eyes. Sure, he wanted to come here to investigate Rev. Alister Cameron's claims, but he didn't want to have dinner with the man.

"You did this on purpose, didn't you? Set this up from the start... probably called the Reverend up while we were still in New York."

"I don't think planning is either of our strong suits," she remarked.

Suzan was standing in the bathroom, applying mascara. For some reason, her eyelashes were connected to her lips; every time she used the tiny brush to apply the mascara, her lips turned downward in an expression that reminded him of a guppy.

So far as Beckett knew, there were no muscles connecting eyelashes and lips, but they most definitely were attached somehow.

Reverend Cameron was right about one thing; there were some mysteries that neither science nor medicine could resolve.

"And you're not going to embarrass me, either," Suzan remarked.

Beckett pulled a T-shirt out of his bag and held it up for her to see in the mirror.

"Does this work?"

Suzan didn't have to say anything; she simply stared.

Beckett looked at his Marilyn Manson T-shirt and shrugged.

"I like it."

"I packed a dress shirt in there for you, a short sleeved one. Wear it."

Suzan used her no-nonsense tone and Beckett groaned. He reached back into the bag and pulled out the shirt she wanted him to wear. It was off-white, practically see-through, and looked about as comfortable as a burlap sack.

He sighed but slipped it on.

"And you're going to bring a bottle of wine, too. And not that cheap shit from the gas station. A nice bottle. I also want you to be polite."

He shifted uncomfortably in his shirt; it looked as comfortable as a burlap sack but felt more like barbed wire against his delicate skin.

"Yes, Mom," he said. "You owe me for this."

Again, Suzan gave him that stare.

"No, Dr. Beckett Campbell, you owe me," she corrected.

***

"Welcome," Rev. Cameron said with a broad smile. He looked almost normal out of his priest regalia and dressed in a button-down shirt and tan-colored slacks. His hair was neatly parted to one side.

"Thanks for having us," Suzan said.

"Of course, *mi casa, su casa*. I'm sorry, but I was never good with names."

"Suzan, Suzan Cuthbert."

Rev. Cameron leaned in and gave her a kiss on the cheek before turning to Beckett.

"And it's a pleasure to see you again, Dr. Campbell."

Beckett shook the man's hand, discomforted by the fact that his was completely swallowed by the other man's massive palm.

"Just Beckett," he said. Then he extended the wine bottle.

The man looked at the bottle with keen interest and smiled.

"A Châteauneuf-du-Pape. Very nice. Come on in."

As they stepped inside the large foyer, a woman sporting an apron appeared from what Beckett assumed was the kitchen. She was petite and pretty, with dark hair that fell just below her ears. She also had piercing blue eyes, but Beckett was more interested in her considerable bust. As she moved toward them, her impressive rack didn't so much as bounce.

Rev. Cameron can cure death and also imbue any woman with implants with the simple flick of his tongue.

"And this is Mrs. Cameron," the Reverend said.

"Holly. My name is Holly."

Beckett leaned in and gave her a kiss on the cheek as Alister had done to Suzan, and somehow invoked the power of the Lord to resist the temptation to look down at her breasts.

As if sensing his moral conundrum, Beckett heard a chirp and his eyes were drawn to a side room. He spotted a white bird cage—one of the cheap plastic kinds—and a yellow budgie inside. Neither fit with the décor and struck him as a little odd.

"You like birds?" he asked.

Rev. Cameron hooked a thumb at Holly.

"My wife does. Personally, not my favorite animal. Too many allergens."

Beckett nodded. He hated birds, himself. They just squawked and shit everywhere.

At least they keep the cage clean, he thought, noting what looked like fresh newsprint on the bottom of the cage.

"Enough about birds; let's have a drink, shall we? Holly, do you mind opening this bottle of wine and letting it aerate? Dr. Beckett has brought a good one."

Holly Cameron nodded and took the bottle from her husband. As she walked back to the kitchen, the big man gestured for them to enter the room to their right.

The smell of freshly cooked chicken filled Beckett's nostrils. His appetite had waned somewhat over the past few months, coinciding with the nasty headaches he'd been getting. But for some reason, the smell that inundated his sense now was particularly intoxicating.

He said as much, and the Reverend nodded.

"Yes, Holly is an excellent cook—you're in for a treat. Can I offer you something to drink before dinner? I've got a wonderful scotch collection."

Beckett looked at Suzan, who shrugged. This wasn't turning out the way he thought it would. He thought this night was going to be stuffy, uncomfortable. Never did scotch make an appearance in his expectations.

"What's your favorite dram?" the Reverend asked Beckett. His expression was kindly enough, but those eyes...

Beckett was suddenly struck with a strong sense of déjà vu.

The man's eyes were so similar to Flo-Ann McEwing's and Winston Trent's, that it was unnerving.

Feeling another headache coming on, Beckett clenched his jaw.

"Are you okay?" Suzan asked, suddenly at his side and reaching for his arm.

"I'm fine," he replied. "As for the scotch, I'll take something peaty."

The Reverend, who was watching him closely, nodded.

"How does Ardbeg work for you? I've got Corryvrecken and Uigeadail."

"Uigeadail is one of my favorites," Beckett said.

"And for you, Suzan?"

"I'm fine for now, thank you."

Rev. Cameron nodded and then walked over to the bar to get Beckett's drink.

"You all right?" Suzan asked quietly, concern etched on her face.

"I'm fine. Likely just the devil coming out of me." Suzan didn't laugh. "Just a headache. I'll pop an Excedrin and be fine."

Suzan seemed unconvinced, but the Reverend returned with the drinks.

"Here you go. I assumed you wanted it neat?"

"You got it," Beckett said, taking the glass. The Reverend had made one for himself and they clinked glasses.

Beckett inhaled deeply as he brought the golden liquid to his nose and took a sip.

It tasted like cigar ash mixed with campfire, and he loved every ounce of it.

"Why don't you come sit with me while Holly finishes the meal," the Reverend offered. "We can talk about our trials and tribulations at medical school. Where did you go, by the way? I attended Brown…"

Chapter 25

DUNBAR LIED; HE WASN'T PLANNING on heading home any time soon.

He was planning on doing some research of his own.

After sucking down two more beers, he once again found himself at the bar, trying to get the attention of the bartender with the handlebar mustache.

Eventually, he came over.

"Yeah? What can I help you with?"

"You can help me with getting another beer," Dunbar said sharply. He tried to keep it together and had done a pretty good job in Yasiv's company. But the man wasn't here to babysit him anymore. "And after you get me a beer, you can tell me more about Wayne Cravat."

"I think it's about time you headed home, Officer," the bartender said, taking a step back.

Dunbar quickly gauged his reach and concluded that the bartender was three or maybe four inches out of his range. Clearly, the man was no rookie.

"I'll leave after I get my beer and after you tell me more about Wayne."

The man shook his head and crossed his arms over his chest. His eyes quickly darted over Dunbar's shoulder before returning to center.

"You're done here. Take off before you do something you might regret."

Dunbar sneered.

"Don't tell me what I'm going to regret," he warned. "Give me my goddamn beer."

It was only now that he realized that he was slurring his words, and Dunbar did his best to speak clearly.

"Just—"

A hand came down on his shoulder and he swatted it away.

"I think he's right, you should take off, sleep it off. You'll think more clearly in the morning."

The man who grabbed him was a stocky fellow with spectacles and slicked-back hair.

"Who the fuck are you?"

Before the man could answer, Dunbar slapped his badge down on the counter.

"I'm NYPD; if you touch me again, I'll—"

The man moved quickly. He reached out and grabbed Dunbar by the arm and dragged him off the stool, slipping him into a half-nelson before he could even take his badge back.

"Let go of me!"

"Go home," the man whispered in his ear.

"I'm a cop, goddamn it! Somebody do something!"

Dunbar struggled against the man's grip, but he was seamlessly transitioned from a half- to a full-nelson before he could break free. As he was dragged toward the door, he realized that several other men had joined the first and were giving him a lending hand.

"So am I," the man said. "Now get the fuck out here."

The door was thrown open and Dunbar was tossed into the street. He fell hard on his ass and grimaced.

"Fuck you!" he shouted, but the men were already heading back into the bar.

Dunbar couldn't believe that these assholes were protecting Wayne, after what he'd done.

"Fuck you! Fuck—"

The man who'd grabbed him suddenly appeared in the doorway again, only this time he was clutching something in his hand.

"Don't show your face here again," he said calmly. Then he tossed the item at Dunbar. It struck him in the cheek, just below his eye.

"Shit," he cursed. He tried to scramble to his feet but staggered and fell back down again. He did, however, manage to grab the thing that had been thrown at him and picked it up. He was going to launch it back, hopefully break a window or something, when he realized it was his badge.

With a grunt, he pulled himself to his feet and staggered.

"Dunbar, what the fuck are you doing? What happened to you... that had nothing to do with this."

And yet, his anger continued to build.

He was more than thirty miles from his home, but he walked the entire way until his feet were shredded and blistered, and his body was soaked with sweat despite the cool air.

Chapter 26

BECKETT DABBED HIS LIPS WITH a napkin, soaking up some of the chicken grease that made them glisten. Then he had a sip of wine. They'd finished his bottle long ago and had moved on to the Reverend's. It was good but paled in comparison to the chicken.

"Holly, the chicken was amazing."

Holly beamed.

"Thank you."

"My family's recipe," the Reverend said with a grin.

"It was fantastic," Suzan concurred.

Another thank you from Holly.

Beckett was surprised at how good a time he was having at the Reverend's place. But why wouldn't he? After all, good food and good drink were two of his favorite things.

So long as they steered clear of the giant water buffalo in the room, they'd be fine.

"I'll clear," Holly offered.

"And I'll help," Suzan said, rising to her feet. As the ladies started toward the kitchen with dishes in hand, Beckett looked at the Reverend with a grin on his own face.

What was the point of having a water buffalo in the room if you weren't going to comment on it? That was like watching a unicorn shit rainbows and not search his butthole for a pot of gold.

"So, quick question: does curing death make you tired? Because, I gotta tell you, autopsies are *exhausting*."

The Reverend shook his head and Beckett thought that he was going to come out and say that he couldn't *really* cure death. That he was speaking facetiously, that he wanted to empower people to help themselves or some such nonsense. But the man stuck to his guns.

"No, no, *I* can't cure death—that's just the press talking—I can only do what the Lord empowers me with."

Yeah, and you are staunchly against such fame, aren't you? You and your hundred-dollar bottles of scotch and lavish living quarters. Whatever happened to being humble, hmm?

"Right, the Lord who chose you as his vessel to perform such miracles. Riddle me this, Reverend, how does a doctor become a priest, anyway? What ever happened to the burden of proof?"

"Throughout history, many doctors have moonlighted as religious scholars. You know, most people think religion and science are discordant ideas, but not me. I think they're one and the same, and I also believe that eventually medicine and science will be able to explain religion."

Explain it? It's already been explained… religion is a crutch for the poor, and a tool for the rich. But first and foremost, it's a business.

"You were always religious, then?"

The Reverend hesitated.

"I always believed that the Lord was always with me, but it wasn't until the event that I decided to devote my life to Him."

Ah, and there it is, Beckett thought. *As usual, when something good happens to us that we don't understand, it's because of God's will. When something bad happens, however, it's because of #humans.*

Beckett had no idea how religion scored the default in this scenario, but he personally blamed spicy tofu for everything, good or bad.

"The event? Like the Big Bang?"

The Reverend chuckled.

"No, not the Big Bang. Holly; Holly was the event."

Suzan suddenly appeared in the room and nudged Beckett away from his plate so that she could collect it. She also gave him a look.

Hey, you wanted to come here.

"You mean..."

The Reverend nodded.

"Yes, my wife Holly. She was sick a couple of years ago. Leukemia. Doctors gave her very little chance of living into her forties. I was involved with everything, of course, and did everything in my power to help her, but modern medicine failed. No matter what we did, she kept getting worse."

Beckett didn't need to hear the rest of the story; he heard it before dozens of times. Hundreds of times.

It was a dangerous line of thinking that had no basis in fact.

"Poor Holly was near death when I decided to turn to the Lord and ask Him to spare her."

"And let me guess: he answered."

The man simply held out his hands as if to say, *she's here, isn't she?*

"I touched her forehead as I prayed, and she was miraculously cured. Three days later, we were back home. It was then that I decided that I could help more people using faith than I could with medicine. That was two and a half years ago. I've saved more than a dozen people that the medical community cast off as dead."

"So you claim," Beckett blurted. He couldn't help himself this time.

"Again, like I said in the church, I respect your cynicism and doubt. But I have proof, my good friend. Would you like to see it?"

Beckett felt a little like someone watching a lap dance that he didn't pay for, but he went along with it.

"Would I? Does the Pope shit in the woods?"

Again, the Reverend just looked at him. If his career as a death curist ever fizzled out, the man still had options as a staring contest champion.

"Of course," Rev. Cameron said. He turned his head and hollered over his shoulder. "Holly, can you please grab the folder of the people I've saved?"

I've saved...

"Yes, Alister."

Why can't Suzan be more like her? Beckett thought with a grin. *Subservient, obedient, giant breasts.*

A few seconds later, Holly appeared at Alister's side with a manila folder in hand. He took it from her, pulled a pair of glasses out of his shirt pocket and put them on. Then he opened and read the first two pages to himself before sliding them over to Beckett.

Beckett had no idea how this would prove anything, but he humored the man. He owed him that much for the scotch, anyway.

The pages were part of a patient file, which, confidentiality rules notwithstanding, portrayed a young woman who was positive for hereditary Creutzfeldt-Jakob disease. The genetic testing was clear: she had a prion protein gene V180I mutation. The next page was for the same patient, only this genetic test revealed no mutation. The mutation results were circled in red pen.

Beckett didn't need to see the other cases; he assumed that these results were consistent.

He slid the pages back across the table.

"You still don't believe, do you?" Rev. Cameron asked.

Beckett considered lying, debated cajoling the man, but it just wasn't in his nature.

"Incredible claims require incredible proof, Reverend. The truth is, you can put whatever name on the top of the page that you want, but these genetic results are from different people. Short of me taking the swabs myself, I'm just not gonna believe it."

The Reverend laughed.

"I thought you would say that. Which is why I am offering you a unique opportunity. You can test my ability to cure people for yourself."

Another surprise.

"Really?"

"Sure. Why don't you come by and visit the parish again tomorrow? I would like to introduce you to my most recent patient. If you feel so inclined, you can do the genetic testing yourself."

Beckett was taken aback by this. Most charlatans kept the recipe to their secret potions to themselves. Otherwise, everyone would know that the tincture they just put under their tongue was a combination of goat semen and eel farts.

"It's only ten thirty; why don't we go check on your patient right now?"

"I appreciate your enthusiasm, Beckett, but tonight is not for medical talk. Not anymore, anyway."

Medical talk? It never was...

"And what, pray tell, is tonight for, then?"

Without answering, the man stood and walked over to the bar.

"Why, drinking, of course. Tonight, is for drinking."

Chapter 27

SGT. YASIV HAD JUST TAKEN up residence behind his desk
with a hot cup of coffee when there was a knock at his office
door.

"Come in."

It was Dunbar.

"Fuck, Dunbar, what happened last night?"

There was a welt beneath the man's right eye, and that side
of his face was swollen. Yasiv knew that it had been a mistake
leaving him there, given his state of mind at the time.

"Got into a little tussle at the bar," Dunbar said matter-of-
factly. "Nothing serious, though."

Yasiv had his reservations based on the injury but decided
not to press.

"Come in and sit down."

Dunbar almost collapsed into the chair across from him.
The man was clearly exhausted.

"Is there something you want to tell me, Dunbar? Because I
already told you about the DA breathing down my neck. Shit,
the man called three times this morning to see if I've found
Wayne yet. If he catches wind of a police officer getting into a
bar fight? He won't hesitate to—"

"I was eleven," Dunbar said in a voice that immediately
caused Yasiv to give the man his full attention. "Boy Scouts;
my third year, the second year I was staying over. It was
pouring rain out and there was a hole in my tent. Water was
pouring in and at first, me and the two other scouts—Darren
Horner and Toby Wentz—thought it was hilarious. But it was
damn cold. After a few minutes, when the rain wouldn't let
up, we ran to the main hall where the staff was sleeping."

Dunbar took a deep breath and Yasiv felt his stomach twist into a knot. He knew where this story was going.

"Listen, Dunbar, I didn't mean to—"

Dunbar suddenly looked up at him, tears in his eyes.

"We went to the main hall where the staff slept and knocked on the door. I was hoping that it would be Mrs. Kimbrell who answered it—she was the nicest Leader and I must say she had a pretty sweet rack, too—but it wasn't; it was Mr. Dennis. Mr. Dennis was the one in charge of swimming lessons. He didn't say much, but nobody really liked him... he never did anything to us, it was just a vibe, you know? Anyways, he answered the door and we told him what happened. He let us in. We wanted to sleep in the cafeteria together—we were still amped up from the excitement—but Mr. Dennis said that it was against the rules. He gave us two options: we could either go back and sleep in the soaking tent or we could sleep with the different counselors. I thought it was a bit weird, but I was only eleven at the time. Anyway, I got paired up with a Leader who was only a teenager. He gave me the bed and slept on the floor. Darren got to stay with Mrs. Kimbrell—lucky bastard—while Toby went with Mr. Dennis. When I woke up the next day, I went to our tent and started to take it apart, try to dry it out. Darren helped, but neither of us could find Toby. We couldn't find Mr. Dennis, either. I asked pretty much every Leader, but they had no idea where he was. And then, when swimming class came around that afternoon, Toby suddenly was there. Only, he didn't look so well."

Dunbar took another deep, hitching breath, and Yasiv waited for the man to continue.

"We asked him what was wrong, but he refused to talk about it. Then at dinner, he said that he'd been up sick the night before and that he still wasn't feeling well. I just remember him being all pale, you know? Toby was the one who was always red in the face, running around, being a goof. But not that night. He was frail almost, frail and—I dunno, twitchy. Mr. Dennis—who wasn't at swim class that afternoon—came by our table and said that Toby might have the flu and that we should steer clear of him. The flu? At camp in the middle of summer? People got beaver fever if they drank too much pond water or got sick from potato salad left out in the sun. But the flu? Anyway, I was closer with Toby than Darren was so when he suddenly got up at dinner and ran to the bathroom, I hurried after him. He was crying in the stall. At first, I was embarrassed for him and didn't want to go in, but eventually, I built up the courage and knocked. I asked if he was okay, and when he said no, I asked if he wanted me to get Mr. Dennis. He just fucking screamed. Just howled. I ran out of there... I was so scared. I just went back to my table and drank my juice box in one sip—I still remember the flavor: Hawaiian Punch. Five minutes later, Toby came out, saying he was sorry. I was so confused, but before I could ask him about it, I had to take a leak. I went to the bathroom and took the exact same stall that Toby had been in. That's when I saw it."

When the man paused to take a breath, Yasiv took the opportunity to cut in.

"Dunbar, if—"

"I saw the blood; the toilet was full of it. Hank, there was blood on the seat, blood on the floor, the water in the bowl was pink. I freaked. I ran to tell Mr. Dennis what I saw and you wanna know what he said to me? The fucking bastard told me that this was normal, that when you get the flu sometimes, there can be a little bit of blood in your stool. Then he pointed out that I'd pissed myself. You see, when I saw the blood, I didn't pull my shorts down far enough. Mr. Dennis took me aside and started to talk about how things like blood in the toilet and pee on your pants could be embarrassing, that if people found out, they'd laugh and make fun of us. I was eleven, man. I didn't say anything. Toby went home that night and I never saw him in person again. In fact, I forgot all about him, until I heard his name on the news nearly ten years later to the day."

Dunbar suddenly cursed and wiped his face with the back of his sleeve.

"Toby committed suicide. Jumped off a fucking bridge. Apparently, he'd been a long-time drug and alcohol abuser. Shit, this whole thing with Wayne Cravat and Winston Trent... it just brought everything back. If I'd just said *something...*"

Yasiv swallowed hard. It was a horrible story, one that made you not want to have kids.

"I'm sorry," he offered, knowing that it was a pathetic response, but he didn't know what else to say.

"No, *I'm* sorry. I'm sorry because I didn't say anything. That little boy Toby was raped by Mr. Dennis and I didn't say a single word—not a single word. That ruined his life, Hank. Drove him to kill himself in the end."

There were tears streaming down the big man's face now, and Yasiv had to look away for fear of him being overcome by emotion as well.

"It's not your fault, Dunbar. It's not your fault; you were just a kid, too. Don't blame yourself."

"Yeah, I was a kid," Dunbar said softly. "But I still should've said something." He cleared his throat. "And now you know why I don't want a guy like Wayne to get away with that shit."

Yasiv stood and grabbed his coat off the rack behind him.

"Nobody should get away with that."

Dunbar's eyebrows lowered.

"Where are you going?"

"*We* are going," Yasiv corrected, placing a hand on the man's shoulder and squeezing tightly. "*We* are going to find Wayne to make sure that he doesn't ruin anyone else's life."

Chapter 28

BECKETT WAS FAIRLY INTOXICATED BY the time they got back to the Airbnb, and his lovemaking with Suzan was predictably sloppy. When they were done—much quicker than he'd anticipated, mind you—they lay in silence, and Suzan traced a line along his bare chest with her finger. She liked to do this often, outlining the contours of his tattoos. When she moved to the lines on his ribs, he instinctively pressed his arm against his side to prevent her access. But he was drunk and so was she; eventually, she pried her way in.

"I like these tattoos best of all," she whispered. Beckett was drifting in and out of sleep now, and he barely heard her. "When are you going to get another one?"

She ran a finger over each of the eight lines and then drew one more after on his bare skin.

"Yeah, I think it's about time you got another one."

Beckett turned his head away from Suzan and closed his eyes. He wouldn't dream tonight, or at least he didn't think so. It wasn't just the booze, but a calm had come over him. A calm that had finally silenced the tingling in his fingers that had returned shortly after Wayne had finally stopped bleeding.

This had happened before, of course; it was something he liked to call the calm before the storm.

And this only happened right after he met someone that he was going to kill.

"One day," Suzan said in such a soft whisper that Beckett wasn't sure if she'd spoken or if he just imagined it, "One day, I think I'll get one too."

Chapter 29

"I'VE NEVER TOLD ANYBODY THAT story before. Not ever."

Yasiv remained silent as he drove. It was clear that Dunbar was mostly using him as part of this cathartic exercise, and he was fine with that. In truth, he wasn't sure what to say. Even with the most heinous crimes he'd investigated, the victims had always been at arm's length. Yasiv wasn't like some of the more seasoned cops who could compartmentalize and fully embrace the term 'victim' so as to avoid calling these people what they really were—human beings, mothers, daughters, sons, fathers—but none of the crimes as of yet had penetrated his personal life.

Until now, that is.

Yasiv considered Dunbar a friend, even though they'd shared little time together outside of work. But, given the fact that his life was almost exclusively devoted to his job now, this passed as friendship.

And he didn't know how to deal with it. Some people might have been able to pass this sort of thing off, say that Dunbar just needed to man up, that he should be grateful that nothing had happened to *him*.

But Yasiv knew better. He'd known Damien Drake, one of the best detectives the NYPD had ever seen, fall apart from PTSD after his partner's murder. It literally consumed the man.

Dunbar needed help; telling his story was a clear indication that he was *begging* for help. And Yasiv wanted to be the person to help him, but the job came first.

They needed to keep it together in order to catch Wayne Cravat and to make sure he didn't hurt any other boys like he had Will Kingston.

Yasiv cleared his throat.

"Harvey Park Church?"

He knew the name of the church but felt the need to say something to break the silence.

"Yeah, on Chevy Chase Road."

Yasiv nodded and took a right. Less than a minute later, he saw the billboard for the church and pulled into the parking lot.

Before exiting the car, however, he turned to his partner.

"You going to be all right in there?"

Dunbar nodded.

"I'll be fine."

His tone was unconvincing, reminiscent of the night previous when he'd ended up with a bruised cheek, but they'd already come all this way.

Yasiv just had to be ready for anything this time.

"Okay, let's see what we can find out about these meetings."

***

"Sgt. Henry Yasiv, NYPD. I was hoping to ask you a few questions about a man we're looking for."

The priest was old, in his mid-seventies at least, and walked incredibly slowly down the hall. But, for some reason, he insisted on continuing to move. It was as if the man believed that the second he stopped putting one leg in front of the other, his heart would take this as a cue to cease pumping.

"I'll help you in any way that I can, Sergeant. But I won't break the trust of any parishioners who have disclosed information to me during confession."

"No, of course not," Yasiv said. "Nor would we expect you to. We're looking for someone, someone we think might be part of this parish. His name is Wayne Cravat."

Yasiv pulled a photograph from his pocket and held it out to the man. He looked at it while continuing to walk.

"Yes, I know Wayne. He's been coming here for the last six months or so."

Yasiv cast a glance over his shoulder at Dunbar, but the man seemed lost in his own world.

Yeah, a church is probably not the best place for a person who has been traumatized by a childhood rape.

He shook his head and tried to remain focused.

"And when is the last time you saw Wayne, Father?"

"Sunday, I believe. He came for a service. Is there something… something wrong?"

"No; we're just trying to locate him, is all."

The priest was entitled to his secrets, and so was he.

"And you haven't heard from him since?"

"No. He's usually here on Mondays, but I didn't see him here this week."

"And what exactly does Wayne do here at the church, Father? Does he interact with kids? Altar boys, that sort of thing?" Dunbar suddenly barked.

Fuck.

"I'm sorry, Father, I—"

"No, no, it's fine," the priest said, brushing off the comment. Clearly, this wasn't the first time that someone had made a remark of this nature. "But I'm afraid that if you want to find out more about Wayne's involvement in the church, you're going to have to ask him."

They'd arrived at a closed door and, at long last, the priest stopped walking.

"I do apologize, but I have an appointment," he said with a leathery smile. "If you have any other questions, please come by after service tomorrow."

Yasiv pulled a business card from his pocket and handed it to the man.

"Thank you for your time, Father. If you do happen to see Wayne, would you please have him contact me?"

The priest took the card and nodded.

"Of course, now, if you'd excuse me…"

Yasiv turned and started back toward the entrance. He had to physically make sure that Dunbar joined him.

On the way out, he passed a bulletin board covered in random messages. Some were inspirational quotes, while others were offers to babysit or dog walk. But one sheet in particular, a blue piece of paper, caught his attention.

As Yasiv walked by, he reached and yanked it off the board and jammed it into his pocket without Dunbar even noticing.

Chapter 30

BECKETT'S HANGOVER WASN'T THAT BAD considering the amount of alcohol he'd consumed the night before. Still, he was far from one hundred percent when he woke up the next morning. The good news was that he could finally attribute his headache to something tangible.

He and Suzan spent the morning walking around a small village they'd found, but his mind really wasn't into it. He kept thinking about Rev. Alister Cameron and how he'd expected to hate the man, given everything that he stood for and his pompous attitude on stage. But the opposite was actually true. Beckett almost *liked* the Reverend, despite not caring for what the man said, and believing even less of it.

The man also had some good scotch, which was always a plus.

Twice, Suzan had asked if he was okay and both times Beckett replied that he was fine. But in reality, he was just going through the motions, as unfair as that was. He couldn't wait to head back to the church and finally prove the Reverend wrong.

Suzan knew, of course; she could read him like a book, which was disconcerting at times, given his extracurricular activities. She used the fact that he was distracted to her advantage and scored several expensive purses before he realized what was going on.

After choking down some greasy fries and a cheeseburger the size of his head, Beckett burped and proclaimed that he would have to go to confession after that meal.

"We're only here a week, Beckett. No way is that enough time for you to confess to all your sins," Suzan remarked with a smile.

After lunch, the crowd at the shopping center thinned and as they drove to the church, they realized why: everyone in the goddamn state seemed to be going to today's sermon.

Beckett couldn't imagine what the place would look like in a week, let alone a month from now. Given the half-dozen overflowing donation boxes that he passed on the way in, however, he assumed that the Reverend would have no problem producing the seed money for a much more 'appropriate' setting for his miracles.

Yet, despite the crowd, Beckett had no problem making his way to the front. These god-fearing parishioners were also tattoo-fearing parishioners, it seemed. They parted to allow him to pass as if his very touch would taint them.

Reverend Alister Cameron opened much like he had the day prior, only this time every aspect of his performance was amped up a notch or two. At one point, Beckett could have sworn that the man actually leaped into the air.

"So much for being humble in the eyes of the Lord," Beckett whispered.

It was as if everyone was in a trance, drawn in by the man's charisma. Shit, even Suzan seemed enthralled by him.

The stark reality was that, simply put, there were people in this world that had the ability to affect others, people who exuded confidence or pheromones or something that made them and what they represented almost irresistible.

And Rev. Cameron definitely had that special quality. He didn't have the ability to cure death, of course, but he had *something*.

Which was why Beckett decided to see how far he could push the man before he broke.

"Please, I need to be saved," Beckett shouted.

Despite the noise, the Reverend homed in on him, a smile on his wide face. Beckett expected the man to ignore him, but that just wasn't in his nature.

Rev. Cameron hopped off the stage and made his way directly toward him.

Oookay...

"I need to be saved," Beckett repeated.

Rev. Cameron shook his head.

"You don't need to be saved, my son," he declared in a booming voice. "You need to be *healed*. Because you are ill, and I am the cure. I will—"

As he spoke, the Reverend reached out with one of his massive hands and gripped Beckett's forehead.

No turning back now.

Beckett went all in, hamming it up as much as possible. He launched his hands into the air as if the Reverend's very touch was electrifying. Suzan had to brace her body against his to prevent him from toppling.

"Beckett, what the hell?" she hissed.

But there was no turning back now.

Beckett's tongue lolled out of his mouth and started flicking up and down as if performing cunnilingus on an apparition.

"*LLl-l-l-ll-l-loooooooll-ll-l-laahhhhhhhh,*" he cried out, "Shihhfff al-l-l-ll loool-l-ll-l praisssssss-s-se a-ll-l-l-l-l-llllaaaaaaaaaah ll-ll-l-lllllloooooll-l-lloolll-l-l."

Others backed away as he continued speaking in tongues, but when his entire body broke into a grand mal seizure, people started to pray for him.

Beckett could barely keep a straight face. Rev. Cameron, however, was like a Stonehenge.

"You will be healed, my son. You will be cured of your ailment, which is *death*," the man proclaimed in a loud voice.

This struck a chord with Beckett, because he was, if nothing else, a harbinger of death.

"F—f-f-f-f—f-f-fffffffoo-o-o-o-o-o-kkkkk-k-kkkk," Beckett's eyes rolled back. "Y-y-y-y-y-y-y-y-y-yoooooooooooo-o-o-o-o-uuu—u-uuu-uu—"

All of a sudden, Rev. Alister Cameron squeezed his forehead. Not hard, but enough so that Beckett clearly noticed a change in pressure.

His tongue suddenly stopped wagging and his entire body became still.

And then he collapsed to the ground.

Beckett was unconscious before his head struck the floor.

Chapter 31

YASIV WAS USUALLY THE FIRST of the morning crew to arrive, but not today. The door to his office was open, and he was surprised to see the district attorney, Mark Trumbo, sitting in the chair behind his desk.

"Mark," Yasiv said tentatively as he stepped into his office and removed his coat. "Did we have a meeting or something?"

Mark stood up. He was a large man, wearing an even larger suit and a tie that almost made it to his belt buckle. Everything about the man screamed authority; he was born to be either a district attorney or the head of a crime syndicate.

"I need an update on the Wayne Cravat case," Mark said.

Yasiv frowned. He'd expected the man to visit, but what he hadn't planned on was it happening this soon.

"I'm working on it. Nobody seems to know where he is, and those that might know something are refusing to talk."

Mark's upper lip curled.

"I've got everyone breathing down on me, demanding that I put this to bed. It's bad enough that we're out there looking for Mark Kruk and Damien Drake, but this child molester? We gotta get this under wraps. I *need* you to find Wayne Cravat."

The fact that the man had mentioned Mark Kruk and Damien Drake in the same context caused Yasiv's blood pressure to rise, but he took a deep breath and calmed himself.

"I'm doing the best I can—we all are. Don't you have enough on your plate with the Steffani Loomis trial?"

Yasiv hadn't meant to say that last part and immediately regretted the words once they'd left his mouth.

But Mark took the comment in stride.

"She cut a deal this morning. Fifteen years. The woman will serve two thirds, no less."

Mark seemed proud of this, but Yasiv wasn't impressed.

Steffani Loomis had been the last remaining board member of ANGUIS Holdings, the group that Drake had committed his life to tracking down.

Fifteen years… and she'll only serve ten.

Yasiv supposed that this was a positive result, given the woman's status and connections. It had been claimed that the United States Justice System is the best in the world, but that only held true if you had money and influence. And Steffani had lots of both.

And yet, fifteen years seemed like a paltry price to pay for the countless lives Steffani and her cohorts had ruined, the people she exploited, the deaths that were on her hands.

The DA suddenly walked over and squeezed his shoulder.

"I'm sure you won't let me down, Henry. I need you to find Wayne." The man's breath reeked of stale coffee.

It never stopped, it seemed; the favors, the back scratching, the outright collusion. Even after all the corruption that had taken place in the NYPD, the wheeling and dealing never stopped. It was as if it had become a hallmark of democracy itself.

Yasiv grumbled something unintelligible, but the DA was already gone. As he stood there, trying to collect himself, Yasiv pulled the blue sheet of paper he'd taken from the church out of his pocket and stared at it. It was an advertisement for a group meeting at the church, one that promised a safe place to talk about PTSD, abuse, pretty much everything under the sun. A meeting that met every night around ten.

The exact sort of thing that a man like Wayne Cravat might frequent.

Yasiv read the ad several times before an idea sprang to his mind.

He spun and left his office, corralling a tired-looking Detective Dunbar along the way.

"Don't bother taking off your coat," he instructed.

Dunbar gave him a look but followed Yasiv to the front doors of 62nd precinct.

"We gonna hit the road?"

Yasiv nodded.

"Yeah, there's a couple of things I think we need to do. First and foremost? Find this fucking Wayne Cravat guy."

Chapter 32

BECKETT STARTLED AWAKE AND IMMEDIATELY tried to sit up. Some sort of cable connected to the back of his hand pulled him back down again.

"What the fuck?"

A familiar face suddenly hovered over him.

"You're back," Suzan said.

Beckett recoiled.

"Are you… are you okay?" he asked.

"What? Am I okay? Are *you* okay?"

Beckett looked around quickly before answering. He was lying in a hospital bed, and the cable connected to his hand was an IV drip. Without hesitating, he yanked it out.

"Amazing," he muttered. "I've just been cured. I… I can't die."

"Jesus, be serious for once, Beckett. You just collapsed out of the blue. You were messing around, talking in tongues, then you just dropped. The doctors are going to do some tests, but I think—"

Beckett tried to sit up, but he got dizzy and slumped back down.

"No, no tests."

"What do you mean, no tests? You just passed out, fell to the ground. At first, I thought it was just part of your stupid act—super clever by the way—but when you didn't wake up…"

Beckett finally managed to sit up and he swung his leg over the side of the bed.

"No tests," he said more assertively. He used the metal railing to rise to his feet. Someone had replaced his rocker T and jeans with a hospital gown, which meant they'd probably already probed and prodded him.

"I'm just hungover and dehydrated. I'll be fine," he said, unsure of whether this was for his benefit or for Suzan's.

A doctor suddenly barged into the room, his head buried in a file.

"Beckett Campbell?" he said without looking up. "I see here that you have elevated—"

"Keep it to yourself, Doc."

The man raised his gaze and then removed his glasses and put them in his pocket.

"I see that you are standing."

"Did you need a medical degree to tell me that?"

"Beckett, please," Suzan implored, touching his shoulder. He pulled away.

"Who gave you permission to run tests on me? Because I certainly didn't."

The doctor was confused by this interaction and looked over at Suzan for guidance. She simply shrugged.

"We did some blood tests; it's procedure."

Beckett growled and started to slip on his shoes before realizing that he had to get out of his dress and put on his clothes first.

"Yeah, trust me, I know the procedure, I probably wrote them. But I didn't ask for 'em, and I don't want 'em."

The doctor slowly and deliberately tucked the folder under his arm and then stared at Beckett with an annoying sheepish expression.

"You collapsed, Beckett. And your girlfriend here has been telling me that you've been suffering from headaches for quite some time."

"You're giving me a headache. Look, I don't mean to be a dick—okay, maybe I do—but I have to get out of here. The good Reverend told me to run some genetic tests on—"

"Rev. Cameron?" the doctor's voice lifted.

"Is there another Reverend around these parts who can heal death?"

The man opened his mouth to reply, but Beckett shook his head.

"Don't answer that. Yeah, I mean Reverend Cameron. Do you know him?"

The doctor nodded.

"Of course, he came to me with some pretty, how should I put this, amazing claims."

Beckett changed his mind; he could spare a minute for this purveyor of the medical arts.

"Do continue."

"Hmm, well, the Reverend came to me claiming that he'd cured several people of genetic conditions that are often fatal. He said that he would be doubted and that he needed proof to back up his claims. He wanted me to run some genetic tests on his... uh... patients before and after he... uh... treated them."

Beckett held his hands out.

"And?"

"So, I did what he asked."

Beckett shook his head. The man's story was incredibly painful to listen to. It was like pulling teeth, like—

"Wait, are you Dr. Blankenship?" Beckett asked, suddenly remembering the name on the patient files that the Reverend had shown him last night.

"Yes, that's me."

"So, you did the testing, you did the buccal swabs yourself?"

"I did," the doctor confirmed.

"Before and after?"

The man sighed.

"I took both the before and after buccal swabs and I personally sent them out for DNA testing to an accredited lab. I don't know what to tell you, Beckett, but the results were not faked. I was skeptical at first, too, but I can assure you the man is no fraud."

For close to a minute, Beckett just stared at the doctor, expecting him to flinch. This had to be a scam.

"Did you get that white coat and stethoscope from a *Brazzers* movie set? What the hell are you talking about? You can't cure Werner Syndrome or hereditary Creutzfeldt-Jakob disease, you know that, right?"

The doctor cocked his head to one side.

"Before the Reverend, I would have agreed with you. In fact, we had another patient with Creutzfeldt-Jakob syndrome not long before the Reverend healed Stacey Winnegar. Come to think of it, we had a patient with Werner Syndrome, as well."

Beckett did some quick mental math. Both conditions were exceedingly rare, but having two people with each in the same small community? What were the odds?

"Were the patients related?"

Dr. Blankenship shook his head.

"No."

It seemed impossible that this was just a coincidence.

"What happened to the people that Alister didn't heal? The ones that the Lord didn't take pity on?"

Dr. Blankenship took a deep breath before answering.

"They died, that's what happened to them; they died."

Chapter 33

"I'M NOT GOING TO HAVE to... you know, talk to anyone, am I?" Dunbar asked as Yasiv drove back to Happy Valley Trailer Park.

Yasiv glanced over at the blue sheet of paper in the man's hands. He could tell that Dunbar was nervous, but he also knew that he was driven to find Wayne Cravat.

"I dunno, I've never been to one of these things, but if the movies are accurate, you won't have to say anything if you don't want to."

Dunbar made a face.

"What do you expect me to get from this meeting, anyway?"

Again, Yasiv shrugged.

"I have no idea—probably nothing. Maybe we'll get lucky, though, and someone will mention something about Wayne, about the fact that he hasn't shown up in a while."

It was a stretch, but it was also worth a shot. Worst case scenario was that Dunbar got some insight into his own problems.

This time, Yasiv didn't stop outside Wayne's trailer and headed to the main office instead. He did, however, glance over at the man's home as he passed. The lights were off, and there was no indication that anyone had been there since Brent Hopper. By all accounts, Wayne had just packed up and left.

The problem with that was that the man worked a minimum wage job at a meatpacking factory. And given his past, it wasn't like Wayne had boatloads of money stashed away and could just take off to an exotic island. The man was pretty much homebound, which meant that either he'd become a nomad or someone was taking justice into their own hands.

This last thought made him glance over at Dunbar again.

This is going to blow up in my face, Yasiv thought. *You shouldn't get Dunbar involved in this.*

But he really didn't have anybody else he could trust, anyone good at their job, anyway.

Yasiv pulled up in front of the trailer marked with a peeling sign that read 'FRONT OFFICE' and got out of the car.

He knocked once on the plastic door before a gravelly voice hollered for him to enter.

The haze of cigarette smoke inside the office was so thick, that Yasiv had to wave his hand in front of his face in order to see anything. Through the haze, he spotted a woman sitting behind a desk with a face like an antique leather recliner and hair like loose stitching. She had glasses on the end of her nose, and a string of cracked beads that ran from the arms around the back of her neck.

"No vacancy," she grumbled.

Yasiv pulled his badge from his belt and held it out to her.

"I said no vacancy," the woman repeated without looking up.

"We're not looking for a trailer, ma'am," he said as politely as possible. The woman sneered but couldn't quite pull off the expression given the paucity of teeth in her mouth.

"What you want?"

"I just have a couple of questions about one of your tenants. It seems that he missed his parole visit earlier in the week."

"I don't know nothin' about that," the woman replied instantly.

Yasiv tried to stem his frustration. The lack of trust for the police in Wayne's small social circle was becoming a common refrain.

"We're looking for Wayne Cravat."

The woman shook her head.

"Look, we just want to know if you've seen him, that's it," Dunbar spoke up.

Normally, Yasiv would've preferred to do the talking, but this time, he took a moment to look around while the manager or whatever she was turned her attention to Dunbar.

The place was an absolute sty, with beer cans scattered across the desk and floor. There was a small kitchen in the back, but the dishes were piled so high, that Yasiv couldn't even see the countertop.

His eyes wandered until they fell on a bulletin board, not unlike the one back at that church. Most of it was covered in crap, but there were two items of note: a blue sheet identical to the one that he'd taken from the church, while the second was a photograph. The photo appeared to have been taken during a Fourth of July ceremony, given by the fireworks in the distance, and the giant American flag in the background. There were maybe a dozen people in the photo, including the peach in front of them now.

Yasiv squinted.

"Huh."

Wayne Cravat was also in the photo, as was Winston Trent. The latter had his arm around Wayne's shoulder, but the gesture didn't appear friendly. If anything, it looked restrictive.

Yasiv subtly nudged Dunbar and pointed at the photo.

"You guys have a big Fourth of July party here?" he asked.

"The biggest party we got."

"What about security cameras? Do you have any security cameras set up around the trailer park?"

The woman's surly expression became intractable.

"This look like the Ritz to you?"

"No, can't say that it does. All right, thank you so much for your help." Yasiv turned to leave when something occurred to him. "One more thing... you said you had no vacancy?"

"That's right, we ain't got no trailers available."

Yasiv thought about this for a moment. Winston Trent had committed suicide more than three months ago.

"What about Trent's trailer? Is that free?"

Again, the woman shook her head.

"No, Winston Trent and Wayne Cravat's trailers are paid up to the end of the year."

Yasiv shot Dunbar a look.

"By who?" he asked.

"Y'all gonna need a warrant for that," she said, crossing her arms over her chest.

"Yeah, sure, thanks again."

Yasiv left the trailer and lit up a smoke.

"You think that's strange? A couple of ex-cons paid up to the end of the year?" he asked as he made his way to the car.

"I don't get the impression that these brainiacs are master investors. What are you thinking?"

"What am I thinking? I'm thinking that someone paid their rent for them, that's what I'm thinking."

Yasiv pictured the photograph of the two men at the Fourth of July festival, Winston Trent squeezing Wayne tightly as if he didn't want to let the man go.

"Why the fuck would someone do that?"

"To keep them quiet, that's why. To make sure that Winston Trent and Wayne Cravat keep their mouths shut."

PART III

Worst Vacation Ever

Chapter 34

"I STILL HAVE THE SCARS on my back from where my father whipped me. And that was nearly thirty-five years ago. Some of them have faded, but the memories of those days will never go away."

Dunbar folded his hands neatly on his lap as he stared at the man who was speaking. There were ten of them in total, all arranged in a semicircle and seated on plastic chairs that one might expect to find in an elementary school. The man leading the group, thankfully not the priest that he and Yasiv had met earlier, claimed to have been abused in multiple orphanages throughout his adolescence, and now devoted his life to two things: The Lord and helping others.

In Dunbar's opinion, all he really did was sit there and listen. But that's really *all* they did. The leader, who had introduced himself as Franklin—not Frank—went around the room and asked if anybody wanted to 'share.' The man speaking now, a man who looked like he'd seen better days, was the first.

Dunbar wasn't sure what he was supposed to get out of this, but he waited until the man finished and then clapped along with everybody else. The next person to speak told them about how he'd made a horrible mistake and had ended up injuring a young boy and his mother. The man didn't explicitly say so, but Dunbar knew that it had been a drunk driving incident.

When he was done, they all clapped again.

"And now, I see that you're new to the group, would you care to introduce yourself?" Franklin asked.

It took Dunbar several seconds to realize that the man was speaking to him. He brought a hand to his chest.

"No, no, I, uhh, I think that I'm just going to listen this time," he replied awkwardly.

Franklin nodded.

"That's perfectly all right. Perhaps you could just give us your name? If you don't feel comfortable giving your actual name, you can make one up. This is a judgment-free zone."

"Dun—" at the last second, Dunbar decided against using his real name. "Toby. My name is Toby."

The man smiled warmly.

"Thank you, Toby. Hopefully, when the time comes, you'll feel like sharing, too." Franklin turned to the man next to Dunbar. "Tommy? Is there anything you'd like to share?"

This went on for the better part of forty minutes, and to Dunbar's surprise, what had begun as a mandatory exercise, actually became something of merit. The people in the room had an array of issues, ranging from serious to benign, but they all had one thing in common: they were all hurting.

And so was Dunbar.

He'd expected that finally opening up to someone about what had happened more than two decades ago would be liberating, but it wasn't. It was like opening an old wound. And yet, he felt compelled to do it again.

After the first round of confessions, the group broke for a coffee break. Dunbar decided to take this opportunity and try to actually do some work, to make some progress in finding Wayne Cravat.

"Hi," Dunbar said as he sidled up next to Franklin. The man was alone; almost everyone else had wandered outside for a smoke.

"Hi, Toby."

"Hey, I, uhh, I just had a question, for you."

The man turned to look at him, stirring the cream in his coffee almost hypnotically.

"I suspected that you might."

The comment caught Dunbar by surprise.

"What do you mean?"

"You're a police officer, right?"

Another surprise.

"It's that obvious?"

Franklin's smile never faltered.

"Yeah, it is. But I think you also belong here." He took the stir stick out of his coffee and sucked the end. "But hey, what do I know?"

Dunbar shrugged this off. He took the mugshot photo of Wayne Cravat out of his pocket and showed it to Franklin.

"Do you know this man?"

"Of course, that's Wayne."

"He used his real name?" Dunbar asked, genuinely surprised.

Franklin shrugged.

"If his real name is Wayne, then sure. Not everyone is hiding from something, Toby."

No, not everyone; but most definitely Wayne Cravat is.

"And when's the last time you saw him?"

"Oh, about a week ago. I expected him here on Monday—
he's always here on Mondays—but he didn't show. I'm
guessing that's why you're here."

Dunbar nodded.

"Yeah, I'm looking for him. Any idea where he might be?"

Franklin looked off to one side.

"Wayne's story is a sad one. He's been through a lot in his
life, made some mistakes, to be sure. But he's been painted
with a brush that I don't think he deserves. You know, people
come here to talk about their mistakes, but often it's the
people out there, people like you, who need to talk. To
forgive."

Dunbar tried his best not to lash out.

*Forgive? The man needs to be forgiven for what he did to Will
Kingston? Does Mr. Dennis deserve forgiveness for ruining Toby's
life?*

I think not.

"You know where he is?" Dunbar asked harshly. "Where
he likes to hang out?"

"Well, not where, but with whom; Wayne used to hang out
with that Winston guy before…" Franklin shook his head. "He
used to hang out with Winston and the other man."

Dunbar had seen the photograph of Wayne and Winston at
the Fourth of July celebration, but this mention of another
man was new.

"You know this other guy's name?"

Franklin snapped his fingers several times as he racked his
brain.

"Ah, I think his name was Brad or Brandon or something
like that. But, I mean, people use aliases here all the time. The
only reason I know that Winston is the other guy's real name
is because I saw him on the news. I encourage people to use

whatever name they want. Sometimes it helps them open up, pretending to be someone else, speaking in the third person, that sort of thing."

Dunbar quickly pulled his phone from his pocket and scrolled to his photos, eventually pulling one up of the man they'd nabbed outside Wayne Cravat's trailer.

"Is this him? Is this the other guy that Wayne hung out with?"

Franklin cocked his head.

"Yeah, that's him."

Dunbar cursed under his breath and slipped the phone back into his pocket.

"Thanks," he said. "I appreciate your help."

With that, Dunbar turned to leave, before the man's voice drew him back.

"Toby?"

"Yeah?"

"If you ever want to talk about anything, you can come back, okay?"

Dunbar frowned.

Not likely, bud.

"Okay, sure. I'll do that."

Chapter 35

"OKAY, OKAY, I'LL DO THE damn test. But you're not staying, Suzan. There's no way I'm letting you watch me bend over and cough… some things just can't be unseen."

Suzan blinked.

"This better not be another trick."

Beckett crossed himself.

"Scout's honor. Go on back to the Airbnb and I'll join you when I'm done here. It's a waste of time anyway."

It took a little more encouragement, but eventually, Suzan reached down and kissed him on the cheek. Then she warned him again that this better not be some sort of lie and left.

"All right, Mr. Campbell—excuse me *Dr.* Campbell—we're going to start with a chest X-ray, followed by an MRI of your brain. Depending on the results, we may also administer a stress test."

Beckett nodded enthusiastically.

"Sure thing. Can I just go relief myself first? I gotta take the Browns to the Super Bowl if you know what I mean."

"Of course—that's fine. It'll take a bit to prepare everything, anyway."

"Thanks, Doc."

The moment the doctor left, Beckett pulled the IV out of his hand a second time, and then quickly got dressed. He opened the door to his room a crack, then peered out. Dr. Blankenship was speaking to a nurse at the nurse's station and pointing in the direction of his room. Beckett leaned back inside, counted to ten, then quickly darted out, closing the door silently behind him. He walked briskly in the opposite direction of the nurse's station, heading straight for a door marked *Employees Only*. The thing about hospitals was that there were plenty of plainclothes doctors wandering the halls. So long as you moved with authority and looked like you knew where you were going, no one really noticed you.

Which is exactly what Beckett did.

He passed through the swinging doors marked *Employees Only* and found himself in another hallway. It took him less than three seconds to locate the storage locker.

"Perfect," he whispered, a smile on his face.

Inside, he found a brand-new lab coat, still in the packaging. He tore the plastic off and then slipped it on over his T-shirt. There were a handful of stethoscopes on the wire shelf as well, but he decided to leave these where they lay. This wasn't an episode of Grey's Anatomy, after all; nobody walked around with those things dangling around their necks. Unless they were a giant douchebag, that is. Beckett was about to leave when he noticed a box on the floor with Dr. Blankenship's name scrawled across the side. Curious, he dropped to a knee and pulled the cardboard tab back.

"Even perfecter."

Inside, there were a dozen unopened buccal swab kits. He shoved a handful into the pocket of his lab coat and then left the equipment locker.

Beckett could've just walked out of the hospital then, but it would be a shame putting his most excellent disguise to waste. Something that Dr. Blankenship had said was still bothering him; there was just no way that this small town could have two people with Werner Syndrome and two with CJD. Especially people who *weren't* related. It just wasn't possible.

As he made his way back to the civilian corridor, he passed an attractive-looking nurse with her head down.

"Excuse me? Excuse me?" Beckett said softly.

The woman looked up, but when she didn't recognize him, her pretty face twisted into a frown.

"Can I help you?"

Beckett scratched his head.

"I'm sorry... I, uh, I don't mean to bother you, but I'm a resident from New York doing a rotation here, but I can't get into the computer system. I've been doing double shifts and, for the life of me, I can't recall my password. Is there any way—is there any way that you might be able to help me out?"

"You're on rotation here with Dr. Blankenship?" the nurse asked.

Beckett cringed.

"Yeah, but he's gonna be pissed if I go to him. He's just so busy with the Reverend, you know? All these genetic cases... I just need to nab a patient history. Can you help me out?" When it looked like the nurse was about to break, Beckett pressed his palms together. "Please?"

The nurse chuckled.

Oh, Beckett, you sly dog you; nobody can resist your charm. Nobody.

"Okay, sure, but let's be quick; I just saw Dr. Blankenship wandering the halls."

The nurse led him in the opposite direction, eventually stopping in front of a computer terminal out in the open.

Ah, you gotta love rural hospitals.

"You can use my login," she said as she started to type. Beckett peered over her shoulder and made note of both her credentials and her password—just in case. "You only need patient information, right?"

Beckett had hoped to score some Vicodin in case his headache returned, but he'd settle for patient data.

"Yeah, three patients; it's for a research project we're working on. You've probably heard of them." He listed off the names from the folder that the Reverend had shown him at dinner.

"Yeah, the 'special' cases. I'm surprised that Dr. Blankenship hasn't published them yet."

"That's what I'm here for," Beckett said with a grin.

The woman pulled up the patient data.

"There's a lot here... you want me to print it out for you?"

"That would be great. If you could, would it be possible to print out the information for the patients with Werner, CJD, and Cystic Fibrosis who weren't fortunate enough to meet with the Reverend in time? Would that be possible? We're planning on using them as a control group."

"Yeah, of course."

Less than five minutes later, Beckett had a stack of paper with all the information he needed to call out the snake oil salesman masquerading as a priest.

"Thank you so much for helping me out. If there's anything I can do, and I mean *anything*..."

The nurse started to blush, and she averted her eyes.

"Well, if there's a spot for a co-author...?"

"Yeah, of course. These papers are padded with everyone's names from the secretary to the uncle no one wants to talk about. I'm sure we can squeeze you in. What's your name?"

"Maria Higgs."

Beckett held out his hand.

"Dr. Holmes," he said. "Nice to meet you."

Chapter 36

EITHER WAYNE HAD BECOME A nomad, or someone was taking justice into their own hands.

The thought resonated with Sgt. Yasiv.

He kept coming back to Winston Trent committing suicide, the only sure-fire way of determining the outcome of your life. The more he thought about it, the less sense it made. Trent was an egomaniac who loved the spotlight, even going so far as to taunt Bentley Thomas's grieving parents in the press. Sure, there was a civil suit pending against him, but that shouldn't have bothered Winston. After all, he didn't have any money to give should he lose the case. But the majority of his legal troubles, the serious ones, were over.

Yasiv pictured the photograph of Wayne and Winston he'd spotted in the manager's trailer. Nothing about Trent suggested that he was a person who would commit suicide.

He was suddenly struck with the unshakable feeling that Winston Trent's suicide and Wayne's disappearance were linked, much like how the two men had been in the photo.

With the hopes that learning more about the former would lead to information concerning the location of the latter, Yasiv decided to spend the morning at the Medical Examiner's office to see what he might be able to dig up.

Once there, he flashed his badge and asked to speak to Beckett.

"I'm sorry, Officer, but Dr. Campbell is on vacation for the next week. Is there someone else you'd like to speak to?"

Yasiv thought about this for a moment.

"You know what? Can you tell me who signed off on Winston Trent's suicide?"

"I don't have access to that information here," the secretary informed him. "But I can put you in touch with someone in the ME's office if you'd like."

Yasiv nodded. He could easily find out this information on his own—it was somewhere in his files—but maybe the ME could provide additional insight.

"Sure, that'd be great."

The secretary picked up the phone, barked a few words, then hung up.

"The office is just down the hall; take the first left and Dr. Nordmeyer will meet you there."

Yasiv thanked the woman and headed in the direction she'd indicated.

After two wrong turns, he found the door marked ME and knocked. A woman with short black hair and mousy features opened it.

"Hi, I'm Sgt. Yasiv of the NYPD."

The woman nodded and allowed him to enter. Then she closed the door behind him.

"Dr. Karen Nordmeyer. The secretary said you're looking for information about Winston Trent's case?"

Yasiv nodded.

"What do you want to know? That case was closed months ago," the woman's stone-faced expression was a clear indication that she wasn't pleased about him visiting and asking questions. Yasiv understood; he wouldn't like it if someone was snooping around his old cases, either.

"I was just hoping that someone could go over the finer details with me. Are you familiar with the case?"

Dr. Nordmeyer crossed her arms over her narrow chest.

"I signed off on it."

Ah, and that's why you don't want to talk about it.

He thought back to another recent case in which the DA had been convinced that Armand Armatridge had been murdered by his wife. It only came out later that the man's death was just a horrible accident. In a city as big as New York, it wasn't uncommon for mistakes to be made. Yasiv just hoped that this wasn't the case with Winston Trent.

"Great, then you're just the person I want to speak to," he said with a smile that wasn't returned. "Is there anything you can remember about the Trent case as being odd? Out of the ordinary?"

"There's nothing ordinary about suicide," Dr. Nordmeyer snapped.

Yasiv quit smiling. He was getting sick and tired of people clamming up on him. No one wanted to talk about Wayne Cravat or Winston Trent or anything at all that might make his life a little easier.

"Yeah, okay, I get it. But was there anything strange about the suicide itself, anything that was out of the ordinary—you know what I mean."

"The only thing weird about that case was Dr. Campbell's insistence to wrap it up quickly."

Yasiv raised an eyebrow.

"Beckett?"

Dr. Nordmeyer nodded.

"Yeah, he's the Senior ME after all." The way she said those words—Senior ME, after all—was a clear tell that she wasn't fond of the man. This didn't strike Yasiv as odd, however, because he knew Beckett could be an asshole. "He said that there would be a media shitstorm if we took our time with that one. Then he said some nonsense about the shoe fitting or whatnot."

"But you were the ME on the case, right?"

Another curt nod.

"So is there anything at all you can remember about it that *didn't* fit." When Dr. Nordmeyer's expression soured, Yasiv decided to take a more direct approach. "Look, I'm not trying to second guess anyone, put doubt in anyone's mind, or anything like that. The truth is, I'm not even interested in Winston Trent; I'm looking for an associate of his by the name of Wayne Cravat. But things keep linking back to Trent's suicide."

Dr. Nordmeyer glared at him for a moment longer, and Yasiv thought that all was lost. But then her face relaxed.

"Well, I'm confident that it was a suicide; all the telltale signs were there. The guy was probably remorseful over what he'd done and decided to finish himself off."

You're wrong about that one, Yasiv thought. Winston Trent was just about the furthest thing from remorseful you could be.

"But now that you mention it, I did find trace amounts of midazolam in his blood."

"Midazolam?"

"Yeah, it's used to relieve anxiety and invoke sleepiness, often as part of an anesthetic cocktail."

"It's an over-the-counter drug?"

Dr. Nordmeyer shook her head emphatically.

"No, of course not; it's a highly controlled substance."

"So how would someone like Winston Trent come across the stuff? I've never heard of it on the streets."

"That's your domain, not mine. But it's a lot harder to get midazolam than it is heroin, I'll tell you that much. Heroin is also cheaper, more effective, and more readily available."

And yet it was in Winston Trent's blood when he committed suicide.

"Anything else that stood out to you?"

"No. That's it. Like I said, all the telltale signs of a suicide were there."

"Okay, thanks for your help."

Dr. Nordmeyer led him to the door, but she was hesitant, as if there was something she wanted to add, but was nervous about saying it for some reason.

"Is there... is there anything I can do for you?" Yasiv asked.

The doctor looked back at her desk.

"If I had something to give you, something that I'm not sure means anything at all but is strange and I need to show somebody, could I do that now? I mean, show you, but anonymously?"

The woman's rambling was so out of character that Yasiv might have been convinced that he was speaking to a completely different person.

She's scared of something, he realized. *Terrified.*

"Yeah, of course—anonymously."

Dr. Nordmeyer hurried back to her desk and took out a folder. She handed it to him, but when Yasiv went to open it, she placed her palm on top.

"Please, not here. Like I said, I don't—I don't know if it means anything, but I figured because you were here..." she let her sentence trail off. "Anonymously, of course."

Yasiv slipped the folder under his arm.

What the hell is this all about?

"Thanks again, Doctor," he said before heading back to his car. He was just about to open the folder when his phone rang.

"Hello?"

It was Dunbar and he didn't sound happy.

"He lied to us. He fucking lied to us."

Yasiv rubbed his temples. He needed a cigarette, and badly.

"Who did, Dunbar? Who lied to us?"

"Brent Hopper, that's who. He was friends with Wayne *and* Winston. He lied to us."

Chapter 37

ARMED WITH THE PRINTOUTS AND a handful of buccal swab kits, Beckett made his way to the nearest bar. He had an hour to kill, which is about the amount of time he estimated Suzan would be expecting him to be undergoing tests.

Beckett grabbed a pint and started going over the file that the pretty nurse had provided him. It took him all of three minutes to figure out what Reverend Cameron was really doing; it was so obvious that he couldn't believe he hadn't seen it before.

The Reverend was simply using a swab from the person who really had the genetic disease as the *before* sample and a swab from a normal, healthy-*ish* person as the *after*.

It really wasn't even that clever.

Beckett sipped his beer and pulled out his phone.

The Reverend claimed to have attended medical school at Brown University, but Beckett couldn't find a record of him in any of the graduating classes.

"Interesting... did the man lie about that, too?"

In fact, he couldn't find a record of the man anywhere in the university at all. Beckett considered the idea that the Reverend hadn't even attended Brown in any capacity, when he stumbled across an article from May 2008.

Med Student Reprimanded for Administering Unsanctioned Treatments.

Beckett would have glossed over the article, but the inlaid photograph caught his attention.

It was a younger, thinner version of Alister. In fact, if it hadn't been for his cold, dead eyes, Beckett might've thought it was someone else.

What added to the confusion was the fact that the man's name wasn't Alister Cameron, but Alfred Cooper.

Intrigued, Beckett read the entire article. The gist of it was that Alfred had been part of a study group that was testing novel gene editing treatments first in yeast, then in rodents. But things were apparently moving too slowly for little Alfred, so he decided to expedite things. The man injected a patient with a slurry of CRISPR DNA sequences without approval. Thankfully, nothing happened to the patient, but poor little Alfred was reprimanded.

It was amazing to Beckett that the man wasn't expelled or sued, but it was Brown after all. If this had happened at a *real* medical school, Alfred or Alister or whatever his name was would likely find himself behind bars.

"Always trying to cut corners, am I right?"

Alister's motivations were crystal clear now, but how the man managed to rope Dr. Blankenship into his scheme was another question entirely.

The doctor struck him as a straight-edge kind of guy, but money could cause any edge to dull. And, judging by the church's coffers that appeared to be bursting at the seams, there was enough of it to go around.

Rev. Cameron might be performing in a small church today, but next month? Next year? Beckett wouldn't be surprised if the man soon had a setup that rivaled some of the largest Evangelical parishes in the South. He'd have a TV show, a book deal, a goddamn cologne named after him.

But Beckett couldn't possibly allow that. It just wasn't right.

"Can I have a shot of Jamison, please," he asked the waitress as she walked by. The woman nodded and then asked him if he wanted a fresh pint, as well.

Beckett checked his watch.

"Sure, why not."

While she went to fetch his drinks, Beckett briefly—*very* briefly—considered just letting this nonsense play itself out; after all, the charade couldn't go on forever. He and Suzan could have a normal vacation, go sightseeing, enjoy themselves like normal people.

But after the shot and second beer, he found himself absently fondling the buccal swabs in his pocket.

Normal people? How boring…

"I could do that," he said to himself. "But then these would go to waste, and I just loathe when people create waste for no reason. I have to do this; I have to do this for the environment."

"I'm sorry?" the waitress asked.

"I said, check please," Beckett replied with a smile.

No, normal just wouldn't cut it. After paying his bill, Beckett went straight to the parish to meet up with his old buddy Rev. Alister Cameron. Or was it Dr. Alfred Cooper?

Meh, he was never good with names, anyway.

Chapter 38

YASIV MET DUNBAR BACK AT 62nd precinct.

"So, you're saying that all three were friends? Trent, Wayne, and Brent?" Yasiv asked.

"Yeah, that's what the man at the meeting told me. When we interviewed Brent, he said he didn't even know Winston Trent."

"I remember," Yasiv said. "Why would he lie about that? I mean, he already admitted to knowing Wayne, it's not like we were going to judge him for the company he kept."

Dunbar was busy typing away at his computer now and didn't answer.

"What are you doing?"

Dunbar hit a few more keys before turning the monitor to show Yasiv.

"Check it out."

Yasiv leaned in close and squinted at the blurry image. It appeared to be some sort of check made out to Happy Valley Trailer Park. The number '212' was scrawled in the notes section, which was Wayne's trailer number.

Dunbar clicked his mouse and another check replaced the first, this one for trailer 116; Trent's trailer.

"Okay, I don't get it," Yasiv said, leaning back and rubbing his eyes.

"Look at who signed the checks, Hank."

Yasiv took another peek, then pulled away.

"Holy shit; Brent Hopper."

Dunbar smiled.

"He signed *all* the checks, dating back to right before Wayne Cravat was arrested."

"Why would Brent be paying Winston and Wayne's rent?" Yasiv asked.

"Remember what you said about someone paying them off?"

Yasiv nodded.

"Well, I guess we found out the *who*. Now we just need to find out the *why*."

Yasiv tapped his chin as he tried to piece it all together.

"Why... why... why... I visited the ME this morning, asked some questions about Trent's suicide. The ME told me something... strange."

Dunbar sat up straight in his chair.

"What? What'd they say?"

"The ME said that while she was convinced that Trent's death was a suicide," Yasiv began, "she found some sort of calming agent in his blood. Something that you can't just buy in a store or get off the streets."

Dunbar blinked three times.

"Oh my God, you think... you think that maybe Brent took out Winston Trent? And that he's responsible for Wayne going missing?"

Yasiv wanted to caution against jumping to conclusions, but Dunbar was too excited to slow down.

"Shit, maybe they were all in on it together, maybe all three of them took part in killing Will Kingston. Winston probably tried to blackmail Brent, and he—"

"Let's not get out of hand here. All we know for certain is that Brent is paying both the other guys' rent."

"And that he lied to us. *And* that Winston Trent was probably murdered."

"I wouldn't go that far."

"Yeah, but it makes sense, doesn't it?"

It was a stretch, but Yasiv had to admit that nothing that Dunbar had said was impossible.

"I don't know. What I do know, however, is that we should bring Brent Hopper back in and have another chat with him."

All of a sudden Dunbar's expression soured.

"Don't say it," Yasiv said glumly.

But Dunbar couldn't resist.

"If we can find him, that is."

Chapter 39

"WE NORMALLY DON'T DO THIS, hold service twice a day, but there is someone here who desperately needs our help," Rev. Cameron announced to the crowd. Thanks to the service's impromptu nature, word hadn't quite gotten around, and the church was less packed, making it easier for Beckett to elbow his way to the front.

"I want you people to put your hands together for a very brave soul. Her name is Brittany Laberge and she was just recently diagnosed with cystic fibrosis."

Beckett shook his head. The man was profiting off the pain and suffering of others. It was reprehensible.

"Cystic fibrosis is a fatal condition and, to be blunt, the traditional outlook for Brittany is not great. The good news is that with the Lord acting through me, I will be able to provide her with a long happy life, free of the disease that has taken so much from her already. Please, everyone put your hands together for Brittany Laberge."

Everybody started cheering, everyone except for Beckett; he was trying not to reach up and throttle the Reverend.

Cystic fibrosis was a terrible, deadly disease for which there was no cure, regardless of the man's claims.

The crowd suddenly moved to one side as two of the Reverend's aids pushed a wheelchair to the front of the church. Then they helped the teenager onto the stage.

She was wheezing terribly and had to continually dab at her mouth to clear it of mucus. Her hair was damp with sweat and hung in strings in front of her pale face.

Rev. Cameron quickly went to her aid, wrapping his big arm around her waist and helping her to the center of the stage. The wheezing was so pronounced that Beckett could hear it from nearly twenty feet away.

Jesus, this is bad. This is really bad.

"Brittany, I want to praise you for your courage in coming here today. It's not easy to be vulnerable in front of all those people, but it is necessary. Before I begin, I must make it clear that it is not I who has the power to cure death, but the Lord who works through me."

With this final sentence, Rev. Alister Cameron closed his eyes.

Beckett grimaced.

Just don't do it… don't do it. This poor girl.

But if he just stood there and did nothing, this girl would be the first of a parade of sick teenagers. Teenagers who were unfit to travel, accompanied by parents who couldn't afford the airfare.

"Fuck," he whispered, before raising his hand high in the air. "Hold it! *Hold it!*"

Rev. Cameron's eyes snapped open and his cold stare eventually met Beckett's.

"May I come and inspect the patient?" Beckett asked, realizing how stupid that sounded, but unable to come up with anything better on the spot. And yet, it was better than collapsing on the ground after speaking in tongues, which he'd done last time.

Rev. Cameron offered a grand sweeping gesture, and the seas parted for Beckett.

Maybe he is the chosen one.

"I want to now welcome Dr. Campbell to the stage. You see, my people, Dr. Campbell is a nonbeliever."

Beckett was surprised by the smattering of boos that followed, but he ignored them. His only concern was this poor girl now.

"Extraordinary claims require extraordinary evidence," he mumbled as he climbed onto the stage.

Peering out at the hostile audience, he wondered if they would chase him and Suzan out of town with pitchforks should he say the wrong thing.

What the fuck are you doing, Beckett?

"Come on now, we are an inclusive faith. I expect that there will be many non-believers out there, people who consider the good work of the Lord just a hoax. But after Dr. Campbell, a well-respected doctor from New York, confirms that what we are doing here is very much real, it will only further legitimize the Lord's work."

Beckett tried not to roll his eyes.

This was theater at its best. And well-respected? *Him?* Dr. Beckett Campbell, ME? Rev. Cameron really was talking out of his ass now.

"Please, offer our guest a hearty welcome."

There was a smattering of half-hearted applause, which Beckett barely acknowledged. He was busy trying to size up Brittany. She was quite sick, and the mucus that dripped from her nose and eyes and mouth was very real.

As was the terrible wheeze that accompanied every breath.

Beckett pulled a buccal swap from his pocket and approached the girl cautiously.

"Brittany, is it all right if I take a swab of your cheek?" he asked. This clearly wasn't the right place to ask for consent, and he probably wasn't even permitted to practice in this State, but what the hell. He was Beckett, after all.

The girl raised her pale blue eyes to Alister for support.

"It's fine, Dr. Campbell. She is fully willing—"

Beckett moved between the Reverend and the girl.

"Brittany? Do you mind?"

Brittany looked at him and nodded.

That was consent enough; besides, it was just a buccal swab.

"Okay, I'm going to need you to open your mouth wide for me. Can you do that?"

Another nod and Brittany opened her mouth. While it wasn't exactly wide, it was sufficient for Beckett to insert the cotton swab. He rubbed it gently on the inside of her left cheek, making sure to do a long sweeping motion to collect as many epithelials as possible. When he pulled the swab out, he saw that he'd gotten plenty; in fact, the tip was coated with mucus and skin cells. He retracted the swab into the case and clicked it closed. Then he slipped it into his pocket.

"Thank you, Brittany."

Beckett turned to the crowd. They were looking at him with confused expressions on their faces, unsure of how to react, whether they should cheer or clap or just do nothing.

They opted for the latter.

All but one; a woman who looked like Suzan suddenly turned around and left the church.

In fact, Beckett was fairly certain that it *was* Suzan.

"How long does this cure take?" he asked Rev. Cameron out of the side of his mouth.

He expected the man to reply with something obtuse, something along the lines of the Lord works on his own timetable or some bullshit, but the man was full of surprises.

"With the others, it was a single day," he said with authority. Then he turned to the crowd, falling seamlessly back into character. "When I touch this poor girl's forehead, the power of the Lord will course through me and I will heal her of her condition. Death, my people, is just a disease, and I am the cure."

And then Rev. Cameron reached out and grasped the girl's forehead. His hand was so large that it almost engulfed her entire head.

An audible gasp ripped through the crowd, and Beckett felt sick just watching this charade. They truly did expect lightning bolts to fly from the Reverend's fingers and zap the cystic fibrosis out of her.

Shaking his head, Beckett slid off the stage and hurried to the door that he'd seen Suzan leave through moments ago. Everyone was so enthralled by the spectacle that they barely noticed him. For some reason, when he was already half outside, Beckett felt inclined to look back one final time.

Rev. Alister Cameron was staring directly at him, his eyes dull like lumps of charcoal.

Beckett shuddered. This wasn't just a charade or a game or some sort of act. There was something sinister going on here, he just wasn't sure what.

Chapter 40

"**WHAT DO YOU KNOW ABOUT** Brent Hopper?" Yasiv asked SVU Detective Crumley.

"Not much, actually. I know that he was an associate of Wilson Trent, that they grew up together. But unlike Trent, Hopper was squeaky clean. About six months ago, he was caught shoplifting a video camera. Got paper and a fine, even though the camera mysteriously went missing. That's pretty much it."

Yasiv indicated for Dunbar to write this down, which he did.

"But he wasn't a suspect or anything like that? In Bentley Thomas's or Will Kinston's murders?"

Crumley shook his head.

"No; he had an alibi for both days."

Yasiv strummed his fingers on the desk.

"You remember off hand what his alibi was?"

Crumley pulled open a drawer and rooted through it, eventually producing a file. He quickly scanned several pages.

"Yeah, it says here that he was at some sort of meeting at a church... Harvey Park Church in Queens. PTSD meeting or something. The guy who runs the show, Franklin Burnett vouched for him."

Yasiv looked over at Dunbar, and his partner stared back. No words were exchanged, but it was clear that Dunbar had met this Franklin Burnett.

And there was yet another connection between the three men: Winston Trent, Brent Hopper, and Wayne Cravat were all friends who attended the same meetings at the church.

Now one was dead, and one was missing.

Which left only Brent Hopper.

"I gotta say, I don't mind helping y'all out, but now the DA is breathing down our necks, wanting us to get somewhere with the Will Kingston case. You guys come across anything that might be helpful?"

Yasiv expected as much. Mark Trumbo was a man on a mission, a man who desperately wanted to keep his job when the public just wanted to clean house.

"Sorry about that."

Crumley shrugged.

"It's all right. Professional hazard."

"Well, we don't know anything for sure," Yasiv began, "but all three men are connected. I think maybe—"

"Our working theory is that Brent Hopper is responsible for killing Winston Trent and for Wayne Cravat's disappearance," Dunbar said excitedly.

Yasiv frowned. That wasn't a working theory, that was wishful thinking.

"Yeah, that's a bit of a stretch," Yasiv interjected, shooting Dunbar a look. "But what we know for certain is that Brent has been paying the other two's rent. Paid up until the end of the year, in fact."

"Sounds like a payoff to me," Crumley admitted.

"Exactly what I was thinking," Dunbar agreed, returning Yasiv's stare.

"So, all three of them murder Will Kingston, but only Wayne is charged with the crime. As a reward for keeping his mouth shut, Brent takes care of his rent. Maybe Winston has some dirt on Brent, so he pays his rent, too. Then Winston asks for more, Brent can't or won't pay, so he kills Winston and makes it look like a suicide. Wayne figures this out, or maybe he wants more money, too, so Brent makes him disappear, as well. That sound about right?"

Yasiv's eyes bulged.

The man hadn't just taken a thread and run with it, he'd tied it to the back of a helicopter and done a tour of the Grand Canyon.

"Well, I—uh—I mean—"

"Yeah, that's exactly it," Dunbar offered.

"It's a stretch, but it's more than we got," Crumley said. "You got eyes on Brent?"

Yasiv knew that Dunbar was glaring at him now, but he didn't take the bait.

"No, we pulled him in for questioning a couple of days ago but cut him loose. Nothing to hold him on. We're trying to locate him now, bring him back in. Put the needle to him."

"What about Wayne's trailer? You search it yet?"

Yasiv shook his head.

"No grounds for a warrant."

"I'll tell you what, even though Wayne was acquitted of Will's murder, he's still part of the case. And now that you've connected him to Winston Trent, I can pull some strings. The DA wants this thing wrapped up, so I'm guessin' I can get a warrant pretty quick."

"Really?"

"Yeah; gimme twenty-four, forty-eight hours and I'll get the warrant."

After being snowballed for days, it was a relief to actually move forward with something, as outlandish as their theory might be.

"Thanks."

"No problem and if anything comes up please keep me appraised, and I'll be sure to do the same."

"Of course," Yasiv said.

They shook hands and then Yasiv and Dunbar left Detective Crumley's office.

Dunbar was smiling and despite knowing better, Yasiv couldn't help but ask why.

"I'm not the type of person to say I told you so, but you heard the man; he's on board with my theory."

"Hmm."

"Oh, and Yasiv?"

Yasiv turned.

"Yeah?"

"I told you so."

Chapter 41

"YOU COULDN'T JUST LET IT go, could you?" Suzan asked the moment Beckett opened the door and stepped inside the Airbnb.

Beckett froze.

"I thought I saw you there. So now you're spying on me, is that it?"

Suzan ignored him.

"What were the results of your tests, Beckett?"

"Oh, nothing serious; my PMS is just acting up, he prescribed some Midol and told me to watch some angsty teen movies."

Suzan threw her arms up in frustration, and Beckett decided to take it easy on her. She was close to her breaking point.

"Sorry, I won't know for a few days." He reconsidered his lie. "Maybe a week. In the meantime, Dr. Blankenship said to drink lots of beer, have lots of sex, and just generally act irresponsibly. I mean, that was just one man's opinion, and I don't know how they teach medicine here in the Carolinas, but quite frankly I'm appalled."

Suzan stared at him.

"Did you mail the damn swab away, at least?"

Beckett grinned.

"I overnighted it to Doogie Houser back in the lab. Grant said he'd submit it to genetic testing right away. Rev. Cameron said his magic touchy-feely thing takes a day, so I'll swab the poor girl again tomorrow. In a couple of days, we'll be able to call him out for the fraud that he is."

"And then what? And then can we have a real vacation? *Please?* You owe me, Beckett. Seriously."

Beckett reached for her, wrapping his arm around her waist and pulling her tight. She tried to push away, but he wouldn't let her. Then he leaned in close and kissed her full on the lips.

"We can start that vacay right now if that's what you want."

"Fat chance of that," she shot back, successfully pulling away. "I need to be wined and dined first."

"So, dinner it is! Taco Bell or Burger King?"

Suzan didn't even turn around.

She's going to kill you, Beckett.

"Kidding! Kidding! Chicken and waffles for the win. And maybe a Shirley Temple for the little lady?"

***

"Wow, that artery-clogging mess was delicious," Beckett exclaimed, licking the gravy off his fingers. Suzan gave him a look and he apologized and used a napkin. But then she giggled and went ahead and licked her own fingers.

They were having a good time, just enjoying each other's company and chatting.

They talked about medicine, about Suzan's plans, and then she started to talk about her mom, about Drake, about her new stepbrother.

Beckett listened mostly. He was a good listener when he wasn't interrupting with sarcasm and jokes, that is. Most of the time, this was a defense mechanism, a tool he used when he didn't know what to say. But with Suzan, he didn't feel the need to say anything. She just got him, understood him in ways that no one else had.

When she was finally done speaking, Suzan blushed and sipped her cocktail. Normally, this would be the time when Beckett made a joke, but he was well into the sauce himself and his guard was down.

"Why are you with me, Suzan?"

The question caught her by surprise, and she looked at him for a moment as if he were playing another one of his games.

"Seriously, why are you with me?"

"Because you have a big—"

Beckett shook his head.

"You're young, smart, beautiful. You're funny and have the patience of the Pope. And yet you're with me: an old man with tattoos and dyed hair and a twisted sense of morality. Why?"

Suzan took her time before answering.

"Because you don't give a shit, Beckett, and yet you care."

Beckett scratched his head.

"Sorry, I was never any good at mental Sudoku. What the hell are you talking about?"

"What I mean, is that you don't give a shit what other people think about you. You're not into Instagram fame, you don't care if other doctors look at you funny because of your hair and tattoos, or because you don't fill the stereotype of what it means to be a doctor. Either people like you, or they don't. You don't lose sleep over it. And in a world where social currency is determined by the number of likes, or shares, or tweets, or twats, you just stick to your guns, to what you think is right. That's the thing, when you care about something, when you believe in something strongly, there's nothing anybody can say—not even me—that can convince you otherwise. I admire that."

Now it was Beckett's turn to blush. He wasn't used to being analyzed in this way and, quite frankly, wasn't sure he liked it. It was too... *revealing.*

"And you got a big dick," Suzan added.

Beckett laughed.

That night he put his considerable member to good use, and they had the best sex of their lives.

Chapter 42

"CIGARETTE LADY IS NOT GOING to be happy that we're back here," Dunbar remarked as they pulled into Happy Valley for the third time in two days.

"Yeah, well, this time we're not gonna tell her, are we?" Yasiv drove past Wayne's trailer and headed to 116: Winston Trent's.

Detective Crumley was still working on getting a warrant to search Wayne's trailer, but Yasiv had flagged Winston Trent's case. A flag wasn't the same as re-opening it—that was something he wasn't keen on doing—but it made the trailer an active crime scene again… sort of. He just hoped that the DA would consider his methodology for gaining access to the man's trailer as creative instead of criminal.

Besides, the man was dead and had no family to speak of. Who would complain?

"Good point," Dunbar replied as they walked up to the door. "What are we looking for, exactly?"

"I have no idea," Yasiv admitted.

The door was predictably locked, Yasiv tried the window in the front. It too wouldn't budge.

"I'll be back," he said to Dunbar as he walked around to the other side of the trailer. The first window he tried opened just wide enough for him to weasel his way inside.

The first thing that hit him was the smell. Winston Trent might be paid up until the end of the year, but after that? Whoever took possession of the place next year was in for a surprise.

Covering his nose and mouth with his shirt, Yasiv made his way to the door and unlocked it.

"Come in, Dunbar. Let's be quick."

The lights didn't work; clearly, Brent's generosity didn't extend to paying the utility bills. Still, there was enough light coming in through the window that they could walk around without tripping over the scattered refuse.

They also had their flashlights, which came in handy.

As Yasiv shone his flashlight at the approximate area that Trent's body had been found, Dunbar focused on the kitchen.

"Hey, you know whose case this was? The first officer on the scene?" Dunbar asked as he sifted through the pots and pans on the counter

"No idea."

Yasiv lowered his flashlight and started scanning the floor. He could see a dark stain where he assumed Winston's blood had pooled.

"Officer Kramer," Dunbar said matter-of-factly. "That's who."

Yasiv looked at his partner.

"Seriously?"

Dunbar nodded.

"Yeah, he was the first one on the scene, called the ME in. His report said it was a suicide, which was later confirmed by the ME."

"Interesting," he muttered under his breath. Officer Kramer was the one who'd pressed charges against Yasiv's old friend and ex-NYPD Detective Damien Drake. "You find anything over there?"

Dunbar banged some pots.

"Nope—nothing."

Yasiv shrugged. He wasn't really sure what he'd hoped to find.

A needle with leftover midazolam in it, perhaps? Maybe a note from the murderer?

Yasiv scolded himself. Dunbar was the one who was grasping at straws, while he was supposed to be the level-headed of the two.

"Yeah, let's just do a quick look in the bedroom and get out of here before—"

Yasiv stopped. The beam of his flashlight had illuminated something by the baseboard leading to the bedroom. It looked like a small section of yarn.

"What? You find something?"

Yasiv didn't answer right away. He bent down and picked up the thread, only it was longer than he expected. It ran beneath the door to a closet, and when he pulled hard, it got stuck.

"Not sure," Yasiv said as he opened the closet. There, attached to the string with some sort of clothespin, was a photograph.

He dusted it off then focused his flashlight on it. Dunbar was suddenly behind him, peering over his shoulder.

"Holy shit, that's Bentley Thomas."

Yasiv nodded.

"That's what I figured. The question is, what the hell is his picture doing in Winston Trent's trailer?"

Chapter 43

SUZAN AND BECKETT WENT FOR breakfast in the morning, and Beckett ordered the exact same thing he had the night before: fried chicken and waffles. He chased it with a Bloody Mary.

Suzan was more conservative, ordering a spinach omelet and a coffee. She looked worse for wear, which was to be expected; she'd drunk more than she usually did and lacked Beckett's constitution.

"You're going this afternoon, aren't you?"

Beckett didn't need her to clarify what she was referring to.

"I gotta see this thing through."

It was explanation enough for Suzan.

Until her third cup of coffee, that is.

"Why does this mean so much to you, anyway? You jealous or something?"

"Of who? Rev. Alister Cameron? I don't think so."

"Then why? I haven't seen you this determined since… well, since those organs just randomly showed up on your desk."

Why am I obsessed with this, you ask? Because there's something wrong with Rev. Alister Cameron. Suzan, when I peer into the face of a killer, I see something in their eyes, a dullness, like a bead that has been massaged with coarse grit sandpaper. How do I know that this means they're a killer? It's because I see the same thing in my own eyes when I stare in the mirror.

"What the man is doing is dangerous."

Suzan made a face.

"How so? I mean, I don't believe any of this nonsense, but at least he's giving these people hope."

"Don't mistake lying outright with giving someone hope. Sure, the people he's 'treating' now are terminally ill, so there's little damage that can be done. But what happens when the parents of a kid with something that's completely curable, decide that instead of using conventional medicine, they want Rev. Douchebag Cameron to heal their child? What about the man who has a urinary tract infection, but rather than getting his dick checked, he comes to the good Reverend to get his head touched? Hmm? A week later, he develops sepsis and dies. What about—"

"All right, all right, I get it," Suzan said. "Jesus, I'm eating."

"What about the—"

Suzan rolled her eyes.

"I get it, Beckett. Man, you just don't stop, do you? Sometimes I wonder how your residents deal with you."

Beckett pictured the six residents wandering the halls blindfolded, desperately trying to find the bathroom.

He smiled.

"Oh, they put up with me because they have to. Because they want to learn from the best."

Thoughts about his residents and the Bird Box Medical Challenge brought him full circle to Wayne Cravat.

The man who was currently rotting away in his basement.

Beckett grabbed his phone and opened the app for his thermostat. He lowered the temperature a few more degrees.

"You almost done?" he asked. "Yeah? Let's get the bill then. Let's do some shopping before we have to go visit the Lord Almighty once more."

Chapter 44

"NO, THERE ARE NO FINGERPRINTS on it—except for yours, of course," the CSU tech informed him.

Yasiv frowned. This didn't make sense, either, but he'd come to expect as much. Nothing about Wayne or Brent or Winston made sense. If this was a souvenir, why weren't Winston's fingerprints all over the damn thing?

The week had started out simply enough—find a man who skipped out on his parole meeting—but had transgressed into a three-man pedophile ring with a staged suicide.

"Can you get anything else from the photo? Like where it came from?" Yasiv asked, grasping at straws now.

The man flipped the paper over and looked at the watermark on the back.

"Sure; it's from the hospital."

Yasiv stared at him.

"What? How do you know it's from the hospital?"

He pointed at the gray watermark that looked like a random series of digits to Yasiv.

"This number here? It's an ascension number. All photographs printed at NYU Hospital have it. I think it's used for billing purposes, not sure though. This one starts with a 'P,' so it's either from Pediatrics, Psychiatric, or Pathology."

Yasiv was so confused that he could barely speak.

Someone printed these at the hospital?

"You sure?"

The man nodded.

"Yeah, my brother had this vascular problem and when they printed out his radiology results, it came on paper like this. That one started with an 'R,' though."

Yasiv thought about this for a moment, before taking the photograph back. He folded it along the pre-existing crease, then slipped it into the evidence bag.

"Thanks, Tony. Think you can do me a favor?"

"What's that?"

"Let's just keep this to ourselves, for the time being, okay?"

"Sure, no problem. Anything else I can help you with?"

Yasiv needed a lot of help with this case, but there's nothing that the CSU tech could do to move things along.

"No, that's okay. Thanks again."

As he was walking out of the lab, Yasiv's phone buzzed and he quickly answered.

"Yeah?"

He expected Dunbar but another man replied.

"Is this Sgt. Yasiv?"

"It is. Who's this?"

"It's Detective Crumley from SVU. I managed to get that warrant you wanted. I can meet you at Wayne Cravat's trailer in fifteen."

Yasiv would have preferred to go in alone, or with only Dunbar, but the man sounded determined.

"Okay, sounds good. I'll just collect Detective Dunbar and meet you there."

Yasiv hung up and immediately dialed Dunbar's number.

"Dunbar? Where you at?"

"I'm staking out Brent Hopper's place with Officer McMahon."

"You have your own car?"

"Yep."

"Good; leave McMahon there and meet me at the station. Crumley came through with the warrant; we're finally going to get into Wayne Cravat's trailer."

Chapter 45

THERE WAS NO POMP AND circumstance this time. Rev. Alister Cameron simply invited Beckett over to his house for the second buccal swab. The first thing that he noticed upon entering the man's house was that the budgie didn't chirp to signal his arrival.

"What happened to the bird?" Beckett asked, noticing that the cage was no longer in the front room.

The Reverend looked at him strangely.

"Oh, that. It died last night. Anyways, it was Holly's bird."

Beckett was confused by the response but forgot all about it once Brittany entered the room. He had to give the Lord credit; the man worked quickly. Less than twenty-four hours ago, the girl had been leaking from her entire face. Now, she looked better. Not perfect, but better.

"As you can see, her body is already starting the healing process," Rev. Cameron said.

Beckett approached Brittany cautiously.

"Are you feeling better?" he asked.

"Much. It's still a little hard to breathe, but it's getting better every hour."

Beckett simply observed for a moment. He would have liked to give her a physical, performed some blood tests, but this clearly wasn't the case.

"You don't mind if I swab your cheek again?"

"No, of course not."

Beckett took out a fresh buccal swab, and Brittany opened wide this time. He repeated the procedure that he'd performed the day before.

He wanted to hang around and talk to her some more, but he also wanted to get the sample into the mail.

The Reverend made the decision easy for him.

"Brittany's tired and she needs her rest. Holly is going to take care of her while she continues to recover."

A not-so-subtle hint that it was time for him to leave.

"I'll be doing an announcement tomorrow at the church if you care to join us. All I ask is that if you have your results by then, to be honest about what you've discovered. I've been nothing but fair to you, Dr. Campbell, I expect that you'll be the same to me."

Well, he certainly doesn't lack for confidence.

Beckett crossed himself.

"I swear to God I will."

"And you look after that girl, too. Suzan, she's a good one. She's a keeper."

Beckett made a face. He wasn't comfortable with any of this, let alone taking relationship advice from a priest who treated his wife like the hired help.

Beckett thanked them both then hurried back to his rental car. From there, he sped to the nearest FedEx office and shipped the sample via Same Day to Grant back in New York.

In less than twenty-four hours, just in time for the Reverend's proclamation, I'll have concrete evidence that he's full of shit.

And Beckett couldn't wait to rub the cocky man's face all up in it.

But for now, he had to take Suzan out, because while the Reverend lied about a lot of things, he wasn't lying when he'd referred to her as a keeper.

Chapter 46

"YOU AGAIN," THE MANAGER CROAKED, smoke pouring out of her throat like some sort of geriatric dragon.

Sgt. Yasiv used the warrant to fan away the toxic air. The funny thing was, even as a smoker himself, he couldn't for the life of him stand the smell of second-hand smoke.

"Yeah, but this time I come bearing gifts. This here is Detective Crumley and you've already met Detective Dunbar," he said, hooking a thumb over his shoulder to the two men standing in the doorway.

"What do you want?"

"This is a search warrant for Wayne Cravat's trailer," Yasiv informed her.

The woman frowned.

"I don't got a key."

"That's all right, I've got a crowbar in my trunk. We won't be long, we just—"

The woman rose to her feet. It was like watching someone unfurl a leather belt that had been left out in the rain.

"Why don't y'all just leave the man alone? Everyone picks on him 'cuz he a little slow. It ain't his fault. Ain't none of this his fault."

"Like I told you last time, lady, we're just trying to find Wayne," Yasiv said. "We don't—"

His eyes drifted up to the Fourth of July photograph again.

"Was it Winston Trent? Was he the one picking on Wayne?"

The woman took a massive haul of her cigarette.

"Him and the other kid. I didn't like neither them boys. They no good. But Wayne different."

Yasiv quickly turned to Dunbar and told him to get his phone out.

"You have a photograph of Brent?"

Instead of answering, Dunbar flipped through his pictures until he found what he was looking for. Then he held it out to the manager.

"Is this the other guy you're talking about?"

The woman put her glasses on her beak-like nose and leaned forward.

Then she crossed her arms over her chest.

"I dunno."

Yasiv had his fill of people not wanting to talk to them.

"Would you just fucking tell me if that's the guy? Gimme a fucking break here."

The woman startled and then nodded.

"Yeah, that's him. Him and Winston they treated Wayne like shit. Tell him to do stuff he don't want to do. Wayne a good kid."

"Yeah, you said that already." Then to Crumley and Dunbar, he added, "Let's go, let's get out of here."

"Don't you go messin' up that trailer, now. Wayne paid up 'til the end of the year, but that's it. If you mess it up I won't..."

Yasiv didn't even bother listening to the old hag. Her usefulness had long since run out.

Chapter 47

"YOU'RE NOT EVEN PAYING ATTENTION at all, are you?" Suzan asked.

Beckett glanced up from his cell phone.

"What did you say?"

She reached over and socked him on the arm.

"Just kidding, I am paying attention. You were talking about your menstrual cycle or something."

"No, you're not, you're like a kid on Christmas morning, waiting to open his gifts. This means that much to you, doesn't it? Proving this asshole wrong?"

Beckett grinned.

"Yep, and I'm not afraid to admit it."

And then, as if Santa Claus himself had been listening, his phone suddenly buzzed. He answered before the first ring had even completed, still grinning at Suzan seated across from him.

"Doogie, tell me what you got."

"Ah, Dr. Campbell? It's Grant McEwing."

Beckett sighed.

"Yeah, I know who it is, dork, your name shows up on the call display. Tell me the good news. Tell me you ran the samples I sent you."

"I did... but there must be some sort of mistake. They're not from the same person."

"What? What do you mean?" Beckett stopped smiling.

"I ran the tests like you asked, checking for the most common mutations in Cystic Fibrosis, including F508del, N1303K, I148T—"

"Fuck, just get to the point, Grant, Jesus."

"Well, the first sample was positive for a mutation in F508del. The second swab was negative. It was completely normal. The samples had to be from different people."

Beckett's eyes bulged.

"You okay?" Suzan asked.

Beckett rocketed to his feet so fast that he almost knocked his chair over in the process.

"You're shitting me. You're joking, right?"

"Dr. Campbell, I thought you'd say that, so I ran the samples twice. Same result: first, positive for CF. The second, negative."

Beckett shook his head, trying to wrap his mind around what Grant was telling him. His first instinct was that it was just a mistake. But Grant McEwing didn't make mistakes; the man just simply didn't. He was a walking savant, the only person in the world with a photographic memory as an adult.

And yet, what he was saying was impossible.

"They switched it," Beckett nearly gasped. "The fucking Reverend tracked down the FedEx guy and switched the samples. That's the only thing that makes sense."

Grant cleared his throat.

"I'm not really sure what—"

"Don't argue with me, boy! The FedEx guy is working for Rev. Cameron."

"Calm down, Beckett," Suzan said.

"I can't calm down; he's done something, that damn Reverend has hacked the results."

"Can I go now, Beckett?"

"Yeah, you can go, Grant. Thanks for doing this for me. Oh, wait, one more question."

"Yes?" Grant asked.

"Are you still wearing your blindfold?"

Before the man could answer, Beckett hung up the phone and then stared at Suzan.

"I don't understand it," he said. "Seriously, I have no idea what the hell happened. Grant told me that the first sample came back positive for genetic markers for CF, but the second was negative. Suzan, I took the swab myself. The kits were brand new, still sealed. What the hell's going on?"

Suzan seemed to be enjoying this, which just frustrated and annoyed Beckett even further.

"You think this is funny?"

She stifled a laugh.

"Yeah, I do. You just can't take it; the Reverend beat you. Shit, he beat death."

"No, he didn't beat me, Suzan. I don't know what he did or how, but somehow he managed to fool the damn buccal swabs."

Suzan crossed her arms.

"I doubt it. Maybe the Reverend just called your buddy Grant and convinced him to lie to you."

"Grant is incapable of lying, he's a robot sent back from the future."

But despite his claim, this struck a chord with Beckett. He fired off a quick text, asking for Grant to take a picture of the genetic results. Almost immediately, he had screenshots of both. And they confirmed what Grant had told him over the phone.

"Well, Grant lied, and he manufactured these genetic results. No, that's not it. I don't know how the hell he did it. But the Reverend did something."

Suzan stood up, still chuckling.

"Where do you think you're going?" Beckett asked. "We need to brainstorm. We need to figure this out. We need to get this guy."

"No," Suzan said as she started towards the door. "What we need to do, is head to the church."

Beckett shook his head.

"No way. No fucking way. I'm not going there, I refuse. I'm not doing it."

Suzan reached over and grabbed Beckett by the arm and dragged him to his feet.

"Yeah, you are. You told the man in front of everybody that if he cured death, you'd praise the Lord. And I'm going to videotape the whole damn thing."

Chapter 48

"I DON'T CARE; TOSS THE entire place if you have to. I want receipts, notes, tickets of any kind. I'll even settle for the man's journal. But we gotta find something," Detective Crumley told them as they entered the trailer.

This was a different man from the one Yasiv had met a couple of days ago, but he didn't mind. The man was friendly and helpful but also got down to business.

As he started to search, his mind wandered back to what the manager had said, about how people took advantage of Wayne. She was the second person to say something like that, and Yasiv knew firsthand how manipulative some people could be.

Is it possible that Winston and Brent somehow coerced Wayne into killing Will Kingston?

It was a stretch, but this whole damn thing was like lukewarm taffy.

"You find anything yet?" Crumley hollered.

"Nothing. I got some comic books—Dogman—but not much else. Oh, I also found this." Dunbar held up a vintage Playboy. "Doubt it was his though, given his taste. This prick doesn't even have a computer."

Yasiv thought about the evidence presented at Wayne's trial; mainly, the videotape.

"Hey, Crumley, did you ever find the original tape of Wayne discovering Will's body?"

Crumley swept his arm across the counter, sending several plates and sets of cutlery to the floor. Yasiv cringed at the loud noise.

"We looked but could never find the source."

Yasiv took the cigarette out of his pack and put it to his lips but didn't light up.

"The guy doesn't have a computer, so I doubt he knows how to upload something to YouTube. Someone else must have done it."

Crumley nodded.

"Yeah, that's the conclusion we came to, as well. It just proved impossible to trace."

Dunbar finished clearing the family room and wandered off to search Wayne's bedroom. When he was out of earshot, Yasiv approached Crumley.

"What's your gut feeling about Wayne, Bob? You think he did it? You think he killed Will Kingston?" Yasiv wasn't fond of this sort of speculation, but he was grasping at straws. Dunbar was certain of Wayne's guilt, and he was on the fence. It was up to Crumley to break the tie.

"I don't know. But... well, there's something wrong with Wayne Cravat. But I don't think this is right for him."

Yasiv nodded and left it at that.

Then he set about searching himself, going through a stack of papers by the phone. Most of it was just ancient TV guides, but there was a bunch of things from Wayne's time in school, as well; old tests, an English paper, other random nonsense.

"Well," Dunbar said emerging from the hallway, a grin on his face. He raised his hand and showed them a video camera, perhaps the only new-looking thing in the entire trailer. "Bob, you might just want to change your mind about Wayne Cravat's guilt."

Chapter 49

"I'M NOT GONNA SAY THAT, Suzan. You're being a dick about this, and don't seem at all concerned about how this guy managed to hack the genetic tests. Like, what the hell! We use this shit to convict murderers, and somehow, he hacked it? This doesn't bother you?" Beckett asked, incredulous.

He had refused to drive to the church, but that hadn't worked; Suzan just took the keys and forced him into the passenger seat.

"You promised you would say it."

"Nuh-uh. What I said was that I would admit that he beat the test, that's it."

Suzan laughed.

"No, I believe your exact words were—"

"Whatever, this is bullshit and you know it."

Suzan laughed again, a sound that was suddenly grating. Under normal circumstance, she had such a cute laugh, but now it was sinister and evil.

"You promised, Beckett. Don't make me take back the things I said about you last night," Suzan warned.

"And what part is that?"

"All of it," she said with a chuckle. "All of it."

For the entire drive to the church, Beckett was trapped in his own head, trying to figure out how *he* might have messed up. It wasn't Grant, it wasn't the buccal swabs, and it wasn't the FedEx guy. So that left him. Somehow, somewhere, Beckett had fucked up.

He suddenly snapped his fingers so loudly that Suzan jumped. Clearly, her mind was occupied as well.

"A twin," he said, with a proud smile. "That's it, I've got it. She has a twin. Brittany Laberge porch has a twin, that's the only way this could have happened. In the church, he used twin A who has cystic fibrosis, and in the Reverend's home, he swapped her out for twin B."

Suzan pulled into the church parking lot, and Beckett couldn't help but notice how swollen it was with cars.

"Really? Like identical twins?"

"Of course, identical twins, I saw them. I couldn't even tell the difference. I—shit. *Shit!*"

"And you're the doctor?"

Beckett immediately knew his error; it was impossible for one identical twin to have CF and not the other.

Duh, simple Mendelian genetics.

He threw up his hands.

"I don't know then. I. Just. Don't. Get. It."

There were no free parking spots, so Suzan pulled over alongside the curb, leaving just enough room so that cars could dangle by if need be.

"It's the power of the Lord, Beckett. It's the power of the Lord."

Before getting out of the car, she leaned over and gave him a big hug. This was so surprising, that Beckett didn't immediately embrace her back.

"What was that for?" he asked as she led the way toward the line of people in the front of the church.

"Oh, I don't know. I just felt like hugging you before you were a broken man. I want to remember what you felt like before your pride was shattered."

Beckett scowled.

"You're enjoying this a little too much, you know that?"

"Oh, I do; trust me, Beckett. I do."

Chapter 50

YASIV STARED AT THE VIDEO camera with wide eyes.

"Didn't you say that Brent Hopper was arrested for stealing a video camera?" he asked. His throat was suddenly very dry.

Crumley nodded.

"Yeah, that's why he was on parole. Where did you find it?"

"Well, everything I've heard about Wayne Cravat suggests that he's like a child, so I looked where every kid keeps the stuff they don't want their parents to see."

"Under the mattress," Yasiv said quickly.

"Under the mattress," Dunbar confirmed.

They all gathered around while Dunbar switched the camera on. Then the detective turned the viewfinder, so they could all see and searched the internal memory. It didn't take long to find what they were looking for: there was only one saved file, a video labeled as 'Will'.

Yasiv's heart started to race.

"Play it," he said hoarsely.

Dunbar was also clearly affected by the discovery, and fearful of what was to come, because it took three times for him to click the play button.

Eventually, he managed, and they were greeted by a solid black screen.

"Is it—"

Yasiv shut up when he heard a voice from the camera's tinny speaker.

"How the fuck you work this thing?"

"Take the lens off, you tool."

Light suddenly filled the aperture as the lens cap was removed. The image was blurry until the iris contracted, and then it focused directly on a man's face.

Brent Hopper's face. The man swatted at the camera.

"Not my face, you idiot."

Whoever was operating the camera swung it to the left, passing the face of another man as he did.

Winston Trent.

"Hey, retard," Winston said, clearly addressing the man holding the camera. "Don't start recording yet. We got a little surprise for you... just you wait."

"A surprise? What kind of surprise?"

Even though Yasiv had never heard Wayne's voice, he knew without a doubt that he was the person holding the camera.

Brent laughed.

"Yeah, you fucking pervert. You gonna love this. Me 'n' Winston got somethin' to show you."

Winston joined in with the man's laughter, and Yasiv suddenly felt sick to his stomach.

"Hey, you're not recording this, are you?" Winston suddenly snapped, growing serious again. He snatched the camera from Wayne and turned it around.

Wayne looked terrified.

"This shit on?" Winston growled. Brent came over and tried to help with the camera, but neither of them could figure it out.

"Here," Wayne said softly. He somehow managed to get the lens cap back on. But Wayne didn't stop recording. There was no video, but there was still sound.

Yasiv's eyes darted to the timestamp, and he saw that the video clip was nearly seven minutes long.

During the entire run time, neither he, Crumley, or Dunbar said a single word. They barely breathed.

It was clear that the three of them were walking through the woods, based on the near-constant crunching of dried leaves.

Every once in a while, either Winston or Brent laughed or uttered some disparaging remark about Wayne.

At one point, Yasiv heard the click of a cigarette lighter.

At about the six-minute mark, the camera jostled as if it was being passed around, and then the lens cap was removed again.

"You gotta film it, Wayne," Brent said. "This is your time to be a star."

"Yeah, only you, Wayne."

Wayne appeared reluctant, but he eventually took the camera from Brent.

And then he started to move. Yasiv could hear Brent whispering directions to Wayne — *turn this way, no over there, look down, idiot* — the entire time.

Eventually, the image focused on a maroon backpack half-buried in the leaves. The name 'Will' was stitched just below the zipper.

Yasiv had to avert his eyes for a moment when the camera was directed at Will Kingston's naked body.

"Move the leaves away from his face," either Winston or Brent hissed.

For some reason, instead of running, Wayne listened to the other men. He brushed the leaves away from Will's face and focused on the boy's milky eyes.

Then the camera flipped around, and Yasiv found himself staring at Wayne. His eyes were wide, and his lips were twisted into an expression that was difficult to describe.

And then the video ended.

Yasiv just stared at the black screen for several moments, breathing heavily.

It was Dunbar who eventually broke the silence.

"He wasn't smiling," the detective said softly. "Wayne wasn't smiling; he was terrified. Terrified of what Brent and Winston were going to do to him."

Crumley cleared his throat.

"We had it wrong," he admitted. "Wayne didn't kill Will, Winston and Brent did."

Yasiv finally understood. The part of the video that had been uploaded started only after Wayne was walking toward the backpack. No one had ever seen the first six minutes. The part in which Winston and Brent incriminated themselves.

Dunbar turned off the camera and then pushed the viewfinder back into to place. It snapped loudly, and Yasiv jumped.

"Let's go," Detective Crumley said, his voice acquiring a more stable timber now. "Let's go get this Brent Hopper and charge him with the murder of Will Kingston."

Chapter 51

"CAN'T WE JUST GO HOME?" Beckett begged. He was sweating, and his headache had returned. "Please, Suzan. Don't make me do this."

Suzan didn't answer. Instead, she just dragged him through the doors of the church, and then proceeded to pull him through the throngs of people all the way to the front. It was slow going, and a dozen times Beckett thought that they would be stopped and that would be the end of it.

But Suzan had particularly sharp elbows, and they made it all the way to the stage.

Beckett felt like shit. He did not want to do this.

But when Rev. Cameron appeared, his eyes seemed to be seeking out Beckett. It was like the man knew, like he knew that Beckett had overnighted the swabs, that he'd gotten the results back, and that he'd cured Brittany Laberge of cystic fibrosis.

That he'd cured death.

"Fuck me," he grumbled as the Reverend pointed at him.

Beckett almost turned and ran at that moment, but Suzan held fast. She was enjoying this, but he couldn't blame her.

She finally found a way to get back at him for all of his petty teasing, his sarcasm, his sheer refusal to be serious.

"Welcome, welcome, everyone!" Rev. Cameron cried as Beckett reluctantly hopped onto the stage. "Before I introduce you to my friend here, I would also ask for Brittany Laberge to join us."

Beckett was looking for the teenager in the wheelchair, but he couldn't find her. What he did see, was a young woman who practically leaped onto the stage.

What the fuck?

When he'd taken the swab yesterday, Brittany looked much better than the day before. But now she looked like she could run a marathon.

Brittany Laberge definitely did not look like someone suffering from cystic fibrosis.

The crowd's cheers intensified and were now punctuated by several shrill whistles.

"Just two days ago," the Reverend shouted over the noise. "Brittany was dying. Conventional medicine gave her only a couple of months to live, but the Lord saved her. The Lord used me as a vessel to heal this young woman!"

The roar was deafening now.

Beckett couldn't believe it. If he didn't do anything to stop it, in a week, Rev. Alister Cameron would become a worldwide phenomenon.

And it was partly his fault.

Eventually, after a half-dozen requests from the Reverend, the crowd quieted.

Beckett was sweating buckets now, and his headache had gone from a dull throb to searing pain behind his eyes.

And his fingers were tingling.

"Please, please, most of you will remember our friend Dr. Beckett Campbell from New York City who arrived with the sole purpose of proving that what I've done here—what the Lord has done—is truly, and verifiably, a miracle."

Oh, for fuck's sake.

"Dr. Campbell, can you please tell everyone what your tests have shown?"

The smug expression that graced the Reverend's face made it difficult for Beckett to resist strangling him right there.

If he can cure death, I wonder if he can stop me from choking the life out of him.

"It's true," he said quietly.

"I'm sorry? I didn't hear you."

"It's true. I did the tests myself. Brittany Laberge *had* cystic fibrosis, but now she doesn't. I don't know how you did it, but you did it."

A hush fell over the crowd, and Rev. Cameron basked in this glory.

"What can I say? The Lord works in mysterious ways."

The crowd erupted again, and Beckett's eyes darted down to Suzan's. She was looking at him, but she wasn't smiling anymore. There was an expression of concern on her face, the same expression that she had had when Beckett was in the hospital.

I must look pretty terrible, he thought. Just then, searing agony shot between his temples.

He swallowed hard and clenched his jaw until the pain eased a little.

The last thing he wanted was to slice through the crowd again, elbow his way through the throngs of sweaty parishioners.

Instead, he slipped behind the Reverend and made his way down the side of the stage. There was a door there, and he slid out without too many people taking notice. They weren't here for him, anyway.

His headache started to clear the moment he stepped outside, but it didn't go away entirely.

Beckett was humiliated, he was sick, but he was also determined.

The Reverend was a fraud, he knew this, as did Suzan, he just had to find a way to prove it.

And what better place to find evidence against the man than where this all started?

Beckett pulled out his phone and opened the Uber app, typing in the hospital address as his destination.

***

"I honestly didn't expect to see you back here, Dr. Campbell," Dr. Blankenship said. He obviously wasn't happy about Beckett sneaking off the way he had, but it was clear that he at least partially expected it.

"Yeah, well, you know..."

The man crossed his arms over his chest and waited for Beckett to continue.

"I have a question for you; have you treated anyone for cystic fibrosis recently? A female teenager, perhaps?"

The man's eyes gave it away: he had.

"I'll answer your question, but only if you submit yourself to a few tests."

Beckett tried to remain neutral.

"The ones you planned for me before?"

The doctor nodded.

"Deal," Beckett said quickly. The man eyed him curiously, then gestured towards one of the vacant rooms. Beckett didn't hesitate; he moved in that direction.

"I'll go prepare the paperwork," Dr. Blankenship said as Beckett opened the door to the room and stepped inside. The man scratched his head, then added, "You're not going to be here when I get back, are you?"

Beckett smiled, and Dr. Blankenship frowned.

We have such a cute repartee, he and I.

The moment the doctor was out of sight, Beckett scurried from the examination room, heading toward the door marked 'Employees Only.' He went directly to the computer terminal and then typed in the username and password of the cute nurse he'd met the other day.

It took him all of thirty-five seconds to find the girl with cystic fibrosis: C.J. Vogel, nineteen years of age, diagnosed three months ago. According to the file, she hadn't returned for any follow-up visits since the initial diagnosis. Brittany Laberge was diagnosed one week later.

He must have switched the samples somehow, Beckett thought for the thousandth time. *But how?*

He was about to log out of the system when he realized that the terminal had a drug dispensing tray. The image of his small black case at the bottom of his luggage flashed in his mind.

Inside was a pair of syringes and a scalpel. The problem was, the syringes were empty.

Beckett quickly navigated to the drug ordering system and punched in a request for midazolam.

He retyped the nurse's password to confirm the order and the tray popped open. Beckett scooped up the vial of midazolam and shoved it in his pocket. As he turned to leave, he noticed a couple of blank patient forms beneath the keyboard bearing Dr. Blankenship's header. He grabbed a few of those, too.

Who knew when they would come in handy?

Then he hurried out of the hospital, hoping to never return.

Chapter 52

AS WITH MOST CRIMINALS, WHEN they survived the first round of interviews, when they thought they'd outsmarted the police, they got cocky; Brent Hopper was no exception.

Which is why it wasn't difficult to find the man and apprehend him.

After work, Brent had gone straight home and had plopped himself in front of the TV with a cold one. When SVU practically broke down the door, the man didn't even put up a fight; these kinds of assholes rarely did.

They preferred to pick on people who were unable to defend themselves.

Like, little boys.

Yasiv's executive decision was to keep Dunbar in the observation room, while he and Detective Crumley interrogated the suspect. Dunbar wasn't pleased about this, but Yasiv refused to budge. He wasn't going to let a temper tantrum spoil what seemed like a slam dunk conviction.

They'd placed the video camera that was confirmed as the one that Brent had stolen months ago in the center of the table. And the moment he laid eyes on it, he knew the gig was up. It was only a matter of time before they broke him.

"Brent Hopper, you've been read your rights and you've waived your right to a lawyer. This interview is being recorded, but I'm sure you won't have a problem with that, given the fact that you seem quite comfortable behind the lens," Crumley began.

Brent grunted something incoherent, but while he was still trying to act tough, it was all a facade.

They knew that Brent and Winston had raped and killed Will Kingston, so it seemed reasonable to assume that Brent was paying the rent to keep them quiet. It was also clear that the whole videotape scenario had been a ruse to set up Wayne Cravat, one that had very nearly worked.

"Play the tape," Crumley instructed, and Yasiv obeyed.

The video started to roll, and Brent immediately looked away.

"No, I don't think so," Crumley said. "You're gonna watch."

Brent was shaking now, and even though he was pretending to look at the viewfinder, it was obvious his eyes were locked on the table in front of it.

Yasiv took the opportunity to speak up.

"This is why you were at Wayne's trailer the other day when we grabbed you, isn't it? It wasn't to check up on Wayne but to try and find the tape. You thought he might've recorded more than what they played during his trial, which is why you paid both him and Winston off. But you couldn't find it, could you?" Brent said nothing, but Yasiv continued, undeterred. "And when you couldn't find it, and they refused to tell you where it was, you killed them. You killed Winston and made it look like a suicide and then you took out Wayne, didn't you?"

Brent suddenly glared at him.

"I didn't kill Winston—I didn't do that. And I had nothing to do with Wayne disappearing, either. Shit, I didn't kill the boy. That was Winston."

Yasiv nodded.

"Yeah, you did. I'm guessing that you didn't know which one of them had the tape, so you took out Winston first, thinking that Wayne would be too scared to talk after that. But then I'm thinking that you got nervous, maybe because Wayne was opening up at the PTSD meetings in the church."

Brent started shaking his head violently.

"No, no, no, no *way*. It was Winston's idea to grab that boy. Not mine. I don't want nothin' to do with that. I-I-I was just there. But I didn't touch him, I swear. An-an—and then Winston said that we're both going down for it unless we could get someone else to take the fall. So, he came up with the idea of the video camera and getting Wayne to record it 'n shit. But I didn't—I don't know what happened to Winston or Wayne. I didn't do nothin'."

The man was on the verge of breaking into tears now.

"We'll let the jury decide what role you had to play in Will Kingston's death. I think this time, though, they're gonna come to a different conclusion than they did with Wayne's case, don't you think, Sgt. Yasiv?" Crumley asked.

Yasiv nodded.

"It's pretty convincing if you ask me. Look, you're going down for the murder and rape of a young boy. What difference does it make if you killed Winston? Shit, if he was responsible for murdering Will, you probably did everyone a favor, no?"

Brent gritted his teeth and closed his eyes.

"No, I didn't kill him. I swear. I didn't kill the boy, either, that was Winston. But there was this guy, he was following Winston around, Wayne, too. I never thought that Winston committed suicide, he wouldn't do that. It was this guy, man. He was like, hunting us, or something. Fuck."

He's rambling now, trying to get out of this impossible jam, Yasiv thought.

"Open your eyes," Crumley demanded.

When Brent just kept muttering, *no, no, no,* and shaking his head with his eyes closed, Crumley grabbed him by the hair and yanked his head up.

Yasiv tensed, ready to walk over and relieve the detective if he went any further. But the tactic worked, Brent opened his eyes just as Will's pale face filled the viewfinder.

And then he broke. The man's body literally collapsed as if his bones had been liquefied. He sobbed uncontrollably, and Yasiv quickly offered him a box of Kleenex.

"I didn't mean to. I thought... I thought we were just gonna mess around with the boy, you know? I didn't even like it, man. But Winston, he-he said that we couldn't let the boy go, that we had to kill him. That he'd seen our faces, so we had to strangle him. I mean, I didn't want to. I didn't want to."

Brent became a blubbering mess.

"And you killed Winston because of it," Yasiv suggested when the man had finally calmed down a little. "You killed Winston because he had this tape, and you were worried he was going to go to the police. Then you dealt with Wayne because you thought he'd come clean about the murder at one of those meetings."

The man sniffed loudly and wiped his nose with the back of his sleeve, even though there were plenty of tissues at his disposal.

Then he looked directly into Yasiv's eyes.

"No, I didn't do that. I swear to *God* I didn't do that. It was someone else, man, I'm telling you, there was someone after us. Someone who knew what we've done."

***

"You think the DA's gonna be satisfied with this?" Crumley asked. Yasiv stared at Brent through the one-way glass.

"Satisfied? He's gonna be ecstatic. Sure, he'll want us to find Wayne Cravat, but this confession is gonna take a lot of the pressure off him, make him look good."

"Maybe he'll break and give us Wayne's body," Crumley suggested.

Yasiv rocked his head from side to side.

"Yeah, maybe."

But he didn't really think so. Brent had already confessed to raping and in the very least being complicit in Will's murder, and yet he still proclaimed his innocence when it came to Winston's death. What did he have to lose?

Maybe Winston really did commit suicide.

"Where'd your partner go?"

Yasiv looked around. He was so wrapped up in his thoughts that he didn't even realize that Dunbar wasn't in the observation room anymore.

"I don't know. Listen, I've got some other stuff I need to get to, if anything about Wayne pops up, I'd appreciate if you'd let me know."

Crumley nodded.

"Of course. Thanks for your help on this case. We might call you if there's a trial and we need you to testify, but I doubt we'll go that far. Brent'll probably plead out. Save the taxpayers some money, you know?"

"Yeah, probably," Yasiv said. "Take care."

It was late, and Sgt. Yasiv knew that he should head home to get some rest. After all, he was exhausted, mentally and physically.

What had started out as a simple manhunt had become something much more involved. And terrible.

But part of him was still torn. It was all that stuff that Brent had said about being followed that was nagging him. He was far from the brightest criminal that Yasiv had come across, and he didn't think the man had it in him to come up with a story like that.

So, what did it mean? Was there really a vigilante out there hunting first Winston, then Wayne and eventually coming for Brent?

Yasiv shook his head and started his car.

Just go home and get some sleep, he told himself. *You'll think more clearly in the morning. Brent's just making this shit up. You'll see.*

Only, when he started to drive, Yasiv soon discovered that he wasn't heading in the direction of his home, but the church.

And he wasn't looking for salvation. Not for himself, anyway.

Chapter 53

BECKETT COULD BARELY SEE STRAIGHT. His head was hurting so much, his headache so severe, that his reality had become a swirling mix of migraine aura and floating shapes. He was fairly certain that he was in some sort of dungeon, complete with large, stone walls and a sandy floor. But the rest was an incomprehensible swash of colors.

He had no idea what time it was, where he was, or how he'd gotten there. The last thing he remembered was leaving the hospital with midazolam in his pocket and CJ Vogel and Brittany Laberge on his mind. The next thing he knew he was... *here.*

Wherever that was.

"Where the fuck am I?"

He half-expected the ether to reply and was mildly disappointed when the only thing he heard was the warped echo of his own voice.

Beckett shook his head and squeezed his eyes closed, trying his best to force away the god-awful headache and remember what led him here.

When he opened his eyes, reality had forced the aura to his periphery.

He wasn't in a dungeon, but some sort of basement, Beckett realized. And it wasn't completely as he'd first thought. For one, there was a staircase leading to a closed door behind him. There was also a window high above that hung open.

Is that how I got in here? Is that—

A sound from behind Beckett made him jump, and he quickly moved away from the shadows. There was something there in the darkness, a table maybe. Squinting heavily, he slowly crept forward.

Rats? I fucking hate rats.

"Hello?"

He slowly reached into his pocket and pulled out his cell phone, intent on using the flashlight.

"Is there someone there?"

Instead of a verbal answer, he heard that clanging sound again. If he didn't know any better, it sounded like chains.

He swallowed hard and took another step forward.

What have you gotten yourself into now, Beckett? What have you —

There was a sudden flurry of movement and Beckett leaped backward. His equilibrium was still off from the headache, however, and he tripped and fell on his ass.

A spindly creature suddenly emerged from the shadows, with long claw-like talons stretching out, desperately trying to grab him.

Something warm and wet struck Beckett in the face and then he screamed.

Chapter 54

THE PTSD MEETING WASN'T SCHEDULED to start until later that evening, but Yasiv got lucky. He found the man that Dunbar had previously described, the man with a mustache and calm demeanor, having a cup of coffee in the hallway.

Yasiv introduced himself, and the man shook his hand.

"Two cops in one week; what'd I do wrong, Officer?" Franklin Burnett said with a wry grin.

Yasiv wasn't in the mood for jokes. Not after what he'd seen.

"Detective Dunbar is a colleague of mine, he's a—"

"—troubled man," Franklin finished for him.

Yasiv nodded.

"Yeah, listen, I, uh, don't want to take up too much of your time. I just had a few questions for you. I'm working a case involving two people that used to attend these meetings: Winston Trent and Wayne Cravat."

"Yeah, your partner was asking about them, too. I liked Wayne." He didn't explicitly state that he *didn't* like Winston, but the implication was there.

"Look, this is gonna sound strange, but was there anyone else that came to one of these meetings around the time that Winston had his, uh, accident? Maybe again last week before Wayne went missing? I know that you must get a lot of people coming and going, but I—"

"There was one guy," Franklin interrupted. "He came twice, around the times you mentioned. Didn't say much. Just sat there. That's not terribly unusual, but the weird thing was? He just kept staring at Winston the whole time. And then when Winston was gone, he stared at Wayne. It was odd, to say the least."

Yasiv nodded. Maybe there was something to what Brent was saying, that there was someone after them.

"And this man, did he give a name?"

"He said his name was H.H. Holmes or something like that. It was clearly a fake."

Yasiv made a mental note of the name.

"Was there anything distinctive about him? Can you describe what he looked like?"

"Sure, he wore a hood most of the time, tried to keep a low profile, you know. Also not unusual, but he had this short, blond hair like it was dyed, and I saw some tattoos on his arms when his sleeves moved up. That's pretty much it. Other than that, he had an average build, mid-thirties, maybe, hard to tell."

Yasiv's forehead suddenly broke out in a cold sweat and his jaw fell open.

"Sergeant? You okay?"

Beckett told me to sign off on Winston's suicide… he said it was better than to let things linger…

"Sergeant?"

Yasiv shook his head and tried to clear his thoughts.

"Sorry," he croaked. He pulled out his cell phone and scrolled through his pictures. Eventually, he found one of Drake with his arm wrapped around Beckett. It was taken around the time that they were searching for Craig Sloan. "Can you… is this him? The man on the right, is this the guy?"

His hand was shaking so badly that he could barely hold the phone steady enough to give Franklin a clear look.

"The man on the right?" Franklin said, leaning in. "Yeah, I think that's him, yeah. Do you know him?"

"Th-thanks," Yasiv stammered as he stumbled away from the man.

His mind and heart racing, combined with his exhaustion, was making him disoriented. Somehow, Yasiv managed to find his car and get in.

This can't be, he thought. *No way... it's not—it's not what it seems.*

Still shaking, Yasiv started his car. Only he still didn't head home.

He went to the bar instead.

Chapter 55

IT WASN'T AN ALIEN OR even some sort of creature.

It was a girl.

A girl who was horribly sick, near death, even, and she was chained to the goddamn wall.

And when she reached for Beckett, it wasn't to maim him or to relieve him of his soul, but in desperation.

"Help me," she croaked. The words were a horrible wet wheeze, and mucus sprayed from her lips and oozed from her nose.

Beckett somehow managed to rise to his feet and he went to her.

Close-up, he could see that she wasn't just near death but knocking on its door. And then it hit him. She was in the very late stages of cystic fibrosis.

"C.J.? C.J. Vogel?" he said softly.

The girl somehow managed a nod, her sweat-drenched hair moving ever so slightly in front of her face.

Beckett looked around, searching for a key to remove the shackle from her pencil-thin throat. His eyes focused on the open window again, and he looked out.

That parking lot... I know that parking lot.

His memories suddenly started flooding back.

After the hospital, he'd come here, to the church. Then he'd waited. He waited for everyone to leave before he broke into the basement, intent on finding out exactly how Rev. Cameron was pulling off his scam.

His headache had been building to a crescendo the entire time and when he'd jumped down through the window, it must have been so bad that he passed out. But now that he was regaining most of his senses, Beckett came to the horrible realization that Reverend Alister Cameron had been keeping C.J. Vogel here the entire time. He had locked her up, denied her palliative treatment, made her final days a living hell.

"Help me," the girl croaked again, reaching for him with ragged fingernails. Blood spilled from her mouth and dribbled down her pale chin.

Beckett wished more than anything that he could help her, that he could cure her of this terrible disease.

That he could do what the Reverend claimed; that he could cure death.

But nobody could do that.

"I'm sorry," he whispered.

The girl collapsed to the ground in a heap. She was so thin that her bones looked like they might pierce through the skin.

Beckett rose to his feet and flicked his phone's flashlight on. C.J. cowered away from the light, and he moved the beam away from her. A table suddenly materialized out of the darkness and he hurried toward it.

He was looking for a key to unshackle the poor girl, but what he found took his breath away.

There was a rusty device that looked like a medical grade cheese slicer lying atop a stack of bloody paper towels.

A dermatome, Beckett thought. He remembered using one during his dermatology rotation. They used it to remove the skin from fattier sections of the body and used them for skin grafts for burn victims. *Why would the Reverend have a dermatome? What purpose—*

Beckett gasped.

"Fuck me."

He didn't even need to see the bottle of skin glue in order for everything to click into place. And then fury threatened to overwhelm him.

"Fucking savage."

It was all there, everything that the Reverend needed to cheat the genetic tests. And it was appalling.

The man was using Dr. Blankenship to identify patients with incurable conditions, like C.J. Vogel's cystic fibrosis. They would come to him, or maybe his wife, and the Reverend would take them to the church, likely under the pretense of being saved. Then he would chain them up.

When he found a suitable surrogate, he would use the dermatome to remove several layers of skin from the inside of C.J.'s mouth.

Beckett thought back to when he first asked Brittany to open wide so that he could take the buccal swab. The Reverend had probably coached her not to say anything or to spread her mouth open too much in fear of the makeshift graft coming loose.

So, when Beckett swabbed Brittany's mouth for skin cells, he was actually rubbing a graft of C.J.'s skin.

But Brittany was sick... she looked *like she had cystic fibrosis. How did the Reverend fake that?*

Beckett scoured the desk, shoving the dermatome off to one side. He noticed it wasn't sitting on a layer of paper towels as he'd first thought, but newsprint.

Newsprint that he recognized from the bottom of the bird cage.

Fuck.

Brittany didn't have cystic fibrosis; she was allergic to birds. The reaction he'd seen was caused by hypersensitivity pneumonitis. Rev. Cameron was probably making her breathe in the bird shit and feathers to induce a reaction, and once he took the allergens away, probably with a shot of corticosteroids, the girl's recovery would be swift.

Brittany had no idea of what was going on, that she never had cystic fibrosis in the first place. The Reverend had tricked her, Dr. Blankenship, and Beckett himself.

"Kill me. Please, kill me."

Beckett whipped around and stared at the poor girl. She was barely able to lift her head and her breathing was so shallow that it was nearly imperceptible.

There was a syringe on the table, and he picked it up, then Beckett loaded it with half of the midazolam he'd stolen from the hospital.

"Please," C.J. groaned as he approached.

She reeked of piss and sweat, but Beckett didn't mind. He dropped to his knees and cradled her head in his lap.

"I'm sorry," he whispered. And then he injected the full dose into a bulging artery in the side of her neck.

C.J.'s eyes went wide, but then they slowly started to close. Beckett waited for her breathing to become more regular, shallow as it was, then covered her nose and mouth with his hand.

She didn't struggle, she didn't even seize. The poor girl just slid silently into the night.

When he no longer detected a pulse, Beckett rose to his feet and brushed himself off. Then he collected the bottle of skin glue from the table and put it into his pocket along with the syringe.

It took him three tries to hoist himself out of the window and onto the lawn. Once there, he wiped the tears from his eyes and dialed a number on his phone.

The Reverend answered on the second ring. His words were slurred, as if he'd had a few drinks, perhaps celebrating his latest conquest.

His latest cure.

"Dr. Campbell, I didn't expect—"

"I'm sorry, Reverend. When I left the church, I didn't mean to embarrass you. It's just—well, I'm confused. I didn't think it was possible, I didn't think you could actually cure these people, but the evidence—"

"It's fine, I completely understand. After all, I am a doctor, too. I know what it's like to need overwhelming evidence to believe something. I'm just glad that you came around."

The man's ego was so great that he couldn't see through Beckett's ruse.

"I'm just confused."

"Would you like to come by for a drink? I've got that great peaty scotch you like. We can talk about it tonight if you want."

Beckett started to smile.

"Yeah, I can do that. I'll be there in ten."

"I look forward to it."

Beckett hung up the phone and then dialed another number.

"Suzan? Yeah, I know you're pissed, but I need a favor. It's important."

Chapter 56

SGT. YASIV WALKED INTO *LOCAL 75* and immediately scanned the interior. Wayne Cravat would come to this bar to drink because he was scared and thought that the cops could protect him. But he wasn't scared of Winston Trent or even Brent Hopper.

He was scared of Beckett... he was terrified of Dr. Beckett Campbell.

Yasiv went straight to the bartender with the handlebar mustache.

"You're not gonna cause trouble like your buddy the other night, are you?"

Yasiv shook his head.

"Beer, please," he managed. Taking a seat at the stool caused things to stop spinning and he got a better look at the bar's patrons. As luck would have it, he found the exact man he was looking for. And, once his beer was delivered, he walked over and slid into the booth across from him.

"Sgt. Yasiv, I didn't expect to see you here."

"Tully, I need to ask you something."

The man scratched his beard.

"Sure, anything," he said, clearly sensing that something was off.

Yasiv chugged half his beer, then pulled up the photograph of Beckett and Drake on his phone. This time he didn't bother struggling to hold it still, he simply gave it over.

"You know either of these guys?"

Salzman looked at the image closely before handing it back.

"The guy on the right; I know him. He's a doctor with the Medical Examiner's Office. Beckett."

Yasiv slumped against the seat cushion.

"He comes in here every once in a while, and he and I shoot the shit. Nice guy. Would never think that he's a doctor, though," Tully offered. "You all right, man? You don't look so good."

Beckett was stalking these men; he'd come here to glean information from Tully Salzman about his parolees, and then hone in on them.

He killed Winston Trent. He printed out a picture of Bentley Thomas and hung it up to taunt the man before he staged his suicide. That was why the paper used for the photo was from the Pathology Department.

And then he told Dr. Nordmeyer to quickly sign off on it being a suicide because no one cared about Winston Trent.

But Wayne... Wayne Cravat was different. Wayne *wasn't* guilty.

Yasiv finished his beer, grumbled a thank you, and hurried out of the bar before Tully could stop him. Then he went back to his office and searched the files on his desk for something specific.

"Where is it?"

There were maybe two dozen files related to Wayne's and Winston's and now Brent's cases, but that wasn't what he was looking for.

"God damn it!"

He slammed his office door closed, and that was when he saw it lying on the floor. Yasiv grabbed it and then opened it.

"Please," he muttered.

In the folder that Dr. Karen Nordmeyer had given him, the one he'd forgotten about, was a photograph of a heavily muscled man that Yasiv didn't recognize at first.

But when he saw the man's name—Bob Bumacher—his memory snapped into focus. The man was responsible, allegedly, for bringing sex slaves from Colombia to New York.

He was the one who drove the yacht. Someone had gotten to him, though; someone had broken into his home and stabbed him multiple times.

But what does this have to do with Beckett?

Yasiv scanned the page until he saw the man's name. He was the ME who had signed off on the man's death. He flipped to the second page where someone had circled a line in red and put the initials KN beside the notation.

Apparently, there was DNA found under Bob Bumacher's fingernails; DNA that matched none other than Dr. Beckett Campbell.

Yasiv had worked enough cases to know that sometimes the ME's DNA found its way onto the victim's body. But never once had he ever heard of the ME's DNA ending up wedged beneath the fingernails of a murder victim.

Yasiv had seen enough. He threw the folder onto his desk and pulled out his cell phone. Only he didn't dial a number for a long time. He just stared at it.

His mind was racing, trying to come up with a rational explanation for all of this. But he couldn't. To him, there was only one way that all of these facts made sense. On their own, they meant nothing, but together…

Under normal circumstances, Yasiv didn't think that he would be able to get a search warrant based on the sketchy evidence he had.

Only there was nothing normal about any of this. And Yasiv knew someone in the Special Victims Unit who had a knack for getting warrants in less than twenty-four hours.

Chapter 57

"Beckett, come on in," a beaming Rev. Alister Cameron said.

Beckett, head hung low, slipped inside the man's home.

"Would you like a drink?"

Beckett nodded, and the Rev. retreated to the bar.

"Same as before? Ardbeg?"

"Yeah, please."

As the man started to pour the drinks, Beckett slipped the syringe from his pocket into his palm.

"You know, I just have a couple of questions for you, about the girls you cured."

The clinking of glasses stopped for a second and Beckett crept forward.

"Go ahead."

"Did they ever come to your home?"

The Reverend turned and smiled.

"Sure. They liked my wife's birds, and my wife liked them."

Beckett took his drink from the big man.

"I figured. Just one more thing."

"Yes?"

"How did you cure C.J. Vogel? That one is bugging me."

The Reverend's smile faltered.

"Excuse me?"

"It's just—" the scotch glass slipped from Beckett's hand and fell to the floor. "—shit! I'm sorry."

Beckett dropped to one knee and the Reverend followed.

"That's okay, Holly will just—"

Beckett thrust upward with the syringe, burying it deep in the man's soft neck. Rev. Cameron was so surprised that he fell on his back. Beckett mounted him, driving the syringe deeper and then pushing the plunger all the way down. Rev. Cameron croaked and tried to buck, but Beckett lowered his weight onto the man's chest.

"What are you doing? What the fuck are you doing?" The Rev. yelled, trying desperately to shake Beckett off.

But Beckett lowered his hips and held on.

After close to a minute, the Reverend's movements started to slow.

"Why are you doing this?"

"Because," Beckett hissed. "God doesn't choose who lives and dies. I do."

Chapter 58

REV. ALISTER CAMERON OPENED HIS eyes. By this point, the midazolam had mostly worn off and he immediately started to struggle.

But Beckett had done his due diligence. The Reverend was large and strong, but Wayne Cravat was also a big man.

He'd made sure that the duct tape that secured the man's wrists and ankles to the swivel chair was solid.

"You had me, you know that?" Beckett said as he entered the room.

The Reverend's wide eyes fell on him and he tried to scream, but his words were muffled by the tape laced across his mouth.

"You had me, and I must admit the whole skin grafting thing? That was pretty fucking good. I mean, it wouldn't have held up forever. Eventually, I would have asked for blood tests, and if that still didn't prove you were a fucking liar, I would've done a full genetic test. But at face value? That was smart."

Beckett was holding a scalpel in one hand and the bottle of skin glue in the other. He weighed each of them. The Reverend started huffing and breathing heavily when he raised the scalpel. Beckett lowered it and held up the skin glue, but this didn't elicit the same visceral reaction.

"That's too bad; trust me that the scalpel would have been the easier way out. You should have picked the scalpel."

Beckett slid the blade back into his case and then put it in his pocket. Then he walked right up next to Alister and knelt before him.

"I'm getting better at this," he said with a hint of pride. "I knew there was something wrong with you the second I saw your photo in the newspaper. I just didn't know you'd gone this far. I didn't know that you deprived those poor kids of any treatment they might need, even if it was palliative. I didn't know you were so *sick*."

Beckett started to remove the top from the skin glue container, and the man tried again to speak.

"Yeah, I don't think so. You see, this isn't my first rodeo, either. I take off that tape, and you'll just beg for your life, say you didn't mean it, say you won't do it again. I've heard it all before and none of it is worth my time."

Beckett walked around behind the Reverend and then grabbed him by the hair.

"Now be a good boy and hold still," he said as he reached down with the skin glue.

But Alister Cameron wasn't a good boy and he thrashed mightily. But he had a good set of blond hair and when Beckett yanked, the man's head went straight.

Beckett jammed the nozzle of the skin glue up the Reverend's right nostril. He squeezed hard, injecting about half a bottle's worth before moving onto his other nostril.

The man tried desperately to snort the glue out, but with his mouth covered, he just leaked snot onto his cheek.

It would take a while for the glue to harden, resulting in a horrible death via suffocation.

And Beckett planned to watch the entire thing.

He walked around to the front of the chair again and squatted. The Reverend's face was starting to turn red.

"You took the—" Beckett stopped when a car pulled into the driveway. "Quiet now."

A car door opened and then closed again, and footsteps made their way toward the house. He heard a key in the lock, and then the door opened.

"Thank you so much for taking me out, I really enjoyed the film," Holly said.

"No problem," Suzan called back. "Now I gotta find out where my deadbeat boyfriend is. Have a good night!"

"You too."

The door closed, and Holly tossed her purse onto a bench. "Alister? You here?"

Suzan started the car and pulled out of the driveway.

"Alister?"

Holly walked to the family room and flicked on the lights.

Her eyes went wide, and she saw Alister strapped to the chair, his face now purple, his eyes bulging and red from the lack of oxygen.

"Alister!" she shouted and ran to him. But the woman only made it three steps before Beckett reached out and snaked an arm around her throat.

"You've been a bad girl, haven't you, Holly," he whispered in her ear, before injecting the rest of the midazolam. "You and your birds."

Beckett was in for a long, tiring night. But it would all be worth it in the end.

Chapter 59

"JESUS, BECKETT, ARE YOU OKAY? You look terrible?" Suzan said as soon as Beckett opened the door to their Airbnb. "When you called and said you were in the hospital, and that I should take the Reverend's wife out to the movies, I thought..."

"Naw, no big deal. I just didn't want you to be alone or to see me like that. After all, *me man, me strong, me take care of woman.*"

He thumped his chest.

"But what happened? Are you okay?"

"Fine, just had another one of those fucking headaches. But the good news is," Beckett held up the sheet of paper with Dr. Blankenship's header on it, "*this.*"

"What the hell is *this*?" Suzan asked, taking the paper from his hand.

"It's from Dr. Blankenship. I went back to him last night to get some stronger stuff for my headaches, and he gave me this." Beckett watched as Suzan scanned the sheet of paper, her lips moving ever so slightly as she read. "Clean bill of health. Said I was just dehydrated and that I had low potassium. Eat a banana, drink water and I'll be all good."

Suzan looked up at him with tears in her eyes, then gave him a big hug.

Beckett chuckled and hugged her back.

"I thought you skipped town after your embarrassing display at the church."

"I'll admit it, I wanted to die. That was the worst."

Suzan pulled away and then noticed his hands.

"Why are your fingernails so dirty?"

"Ah, you know, these rural hospitals, they make you take out your own bedpans."

Suzan mock-gagged and Beckett suddenly grew serious.

"What do you say we go home, Suzan? I'm tired, and I don't think I like this place very much."

Suzan smirked.

"I don't like it much here, either, to be honest. And if we stay any longer, you're going to be admitted to the hospital for coronary artery disease from all the chicken and waffles you've been eating. I think we should get on a flight outta town this afternoon."

Beckett nodded.

"Sounds good to me."

"But," Suzan said, raising a finger.

"But what?"

"You still owe me a vacation. This bullshit doesn't count. And next time? I'm picking the location. I'm picking the location, the accommodations, and you're footing the bill. Got it?"

Beckett smiled.

"Sounds good, boss. Sounds good."

***

"I told your partner, that Yasiv fellow, all I know—don't really have anything to say," Franklin exclaimed as Detective Dunbar approached.

Detective Dunbar looked around, confused.

"No, I… I just…"

Franklin's face suddenly softened, and he reached out to Dunbar. He put an arm around his shoulders, guiding him towards the door. Through the glass, Dunbar could see that half the chairs were filled already.

"I'm sorry, Toby, I thought you were coming for something else."

Dunbar looked up at him.

"My name's not Toby," he said quietly. "My name's Steve, Steve Dunbar. But everyone just calls me Dunbar."

Franklin nodded and opened the door to the room.

"Okay, Dunbar."

"Can I join you guys? I've got a lot of things I need to talk about."

"Of course, you can. We're open to anybody here. Take your time, and when you're ready to speak, we'll be here to listen."

Epilogue

"You're not gonna believe this," Suzan said as she stepped out of the Uber, cell phone in hand.

Beckett was bogged down by bags and struggled to follow her.

"What? What is it?"

Suzan held the cell phone out to him, and Beckett read the title of the article out loud.

"Local Rev. cannot cure death, but he may have caused it."

Beckett raised an eyebrow and Suzan pulled the phone back and began paraphrasing.

"This is... unbelievable. Check this out: Early Tuesday morning, police were called to the church after someone noticed a light left on in the basement. After investigating, they found the remains of C.J. Vogel, a young woman who had been suffering from cystic fibrosis. C.J. had gone missing more than three weeks ago and the police were disturbed to find her chained to the wall. Investigators have been unable to locate either Reverend Alister Cameron or his wife Holly Cameron, who are considered dangerous. If you know anything about their whereabouts please contact local PD. Jesus, Beckett! I was with Holly last night!"

Beckett shifted the bags to one shoulder and unlocked the door to his house.

"I told you he was bad," he said. "I told you that asshole was—"

She punched him on the shoulder.

"Don't talk like that, Beckett. The poor girl is dead. I just can't believe... we had dinner in their house, Beckett. I feel— oh my God—this is just—"

She was cut off by the sound of a car pulling up to the bottom of the driveway. Beckett finally threw the door wide and turned to see who it was.

Two men stepped from a dark vehicle, one of whom he immediately recognized.

"Hank? What's going on?" Beckett hollered.

When the man didn't answer, Beckett instinctively turned his body to block the open door.

"Hank?"

His first thought was that maybe something happened to Drake, or to Screech, or any one of the misfits who were masquerading as private investigators.

But when Yasiv refused to meet his gaze, Beckett's heart started to race in his chest.

The other man, someone he'd never seen before, strode right up to them with a sheet of paper in his hand.

"Dr. Beckett Campbell?"

Beckett's eyes narrowed.

"Yeah, that's me. What's this—"

The man thrust the paper at his chest and Beckett had to drop a bag in order to grab it.

"Hey, what the hell?" Suzan yelled. "Hank, what the fuck is—"

Yasiv averted his eyes.

"Beckett, if you don't get out of the way," he said in a quiet voice, "we're going to have to put you in handcuffs. Please, don't make this any more difficult than it already is. That sheet of paper in your hand is a search warrant—it's a search warrant for your house, Beckett. Now move; we're going inside."

END

Author's Note

BECKETT'S PROBABLY THE MOST FUN character to write, mostly because he can say and do whatever he wants and get away with it. Until now, that is…

But he's also complicated; clearly, he believes his actions are justified, but he often oversteps moral boundaries. They are—how can I put this delicately—*fluid* when it comes to right and wrong. Add Suzan into the mix, who's destined to take a more prominent role in future books, and you've got a recipe for disaster… or hilarity.

Meh, a lot of both.

Join Suzan and Beckett as they continue their adventures through the winding intestinal tract of modern ethics that they seem to make up as they go along.

You can grab the third book in the series – *Surgical Precision* – right now!

You keep reading, and I'll keep writing.

Best,
Patrick
Montreal, 2019

Made in the USA
Coppell, TX
21 February 2020